The Lake of Tears

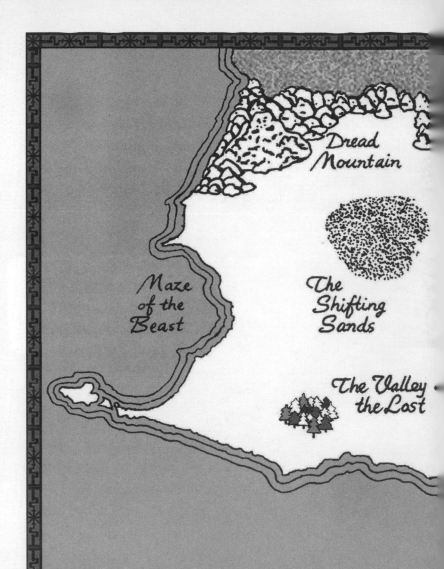

Dread
Mountain

Maze
of the
Beast

The
Shifting
Sands

The Valley
the Lost

THE LAND OF

The Shadowlands

The Lake
of Tears

City
of the
Rats

The Forests
of Silence

Del

DELTORA

N
W · · E
S

VENTURE INTO DELTORA

1 ✳ *The Forests of Silence*

2 ✳ *The Lake of Tears*

3 ✳ *City of the Rats*

4 ✳ *The Shifting Sands*

5 ✳ *Dread Mountain*

6 ✳ *The Maze of the Beast*

7 ✳ *The Valley of the Lost*

8 ✳ *Return to Del*

The Lake of Tears

EMILY RODDA

Scholastic Inc.

New York   Toronto   London   Auckland   Sydney
Mexico City   New Delhi   Hong Kong

ISBN 0-439-81694-7

12 11 10 9 8 7 6 5 4 3 2 1   5 6 7 8 9 10/0

Printed in the U.S.A.
First American continuity edition, November 2005

Contents

1 The Bridge 1

2 Three Questions 6

3 Truth and Lies 12

4 Rescue 21

5 Terror 28

6 Nij and Doj 38

7 Shocks 46

8 Eyes Wide Open 54

9 Stepping Stones 62

10 Quick Thinking 71

11 To Raladin 80

12 Music 89

13 The Lake of Tears 97

14 Soldeen 106

15 The Sorceress 113

16 Fight for Freedom 122

The story so far . . .

Sixteen-year-old Lief, fulfilling a pledge made by his father before he was born, has set out on a great quest to find the seven gems of the magic Belt of Deltora. The Belt is all that can save the kingdom from the tyranny of the evil Shadow Lord, who, only months before Lief's birth, invaded Deltora and enslaved its people with the help of sorcery and his fearsome Grey Guards.

The gems — an amethyst, a topaz, a diamond, a ruby, an opal, a lapis lazuli, and an emerald — were stolen to open the way for the evil Shadow Lord to invade the kingdom. Now they lie hidden in dark and terrible places throughout the land. Only when they have been restored to the Belt can the heir to Deltora's throne be found, and the Shadow Lord's tyranny ended.

Lief set out with one companion — the man Barda, who was once a Palace guard. Now they have been joined by Jasmine — a wild, orphaned girl of Lief's own age, who they met during their first adventure in the fearful Forests of Silence.

In the Forests they discovered the amazing healing powers of the nectar of the Lilies of Life. They also succeeded in finding the first gem — the golden topaz, symbol of faithfulness, which has the power to bring the living into contact with the spirit world, as well as other powers they do not yet understand.

Now read on . . .

1 - The Bridge

Lief, Barda, and Jasmine walked through the crisp, bright morning. The sky was palest blue. The sun slanted between the trees, lighting with bars of gold the winding path they trod. The dark terrors of the Forests of Silence were far behind them.

On such a day, Lief thought, striding along behind Barda, it would be easy to believe that all was well in Deltora. Away from the crowded, ruined city of Del, away from the sight of patroling Grey Guards and the misery of people living in hunger and fear, you could almost forget that the Shadow Lord ruled in the land.

But it would be foolish to forget. The countryside was beautiful, but danger lurked everywhere on the road to the Lake of Tears.

Lief glanced behind him and met Jasmine's eyes.

Jasmine had not wanted to come this way. She had argued against it with all her strength.

Now she walked as lightly and silently as always, but her body was stiff and her mouth was set in a straight, hard line. This morning she had tied her long hair back with a strip of cloth torn from her ragged clothes. Without its usual frame of wild brown curls her face seemed very small and pale and her green eyes looked huge.

The little furry creature she called Filli was clinging to her shoulder, chattering nervously. Kree, the raven, was fluttering clumsily through the trees beside her as if unwilling to keep to the ground but also unwilling to fly too far ahead.

And in that moment Lief realized, with a shock, just how afraid they were.

But Jasmine was so brave in the Forests, he thought, turning quickly back to face the front. She risked her life to save us. This part of Deltora is dangerous, certainly. But then, in these days of the Shadow Lord there is danger everywhere. What is so special about this place? Is there something she has not told us?

He remembered the argument that had taken place as the three companions had discussed where they would go after they left the Forests of Silence.

"It is madness to go through the land to the north!" Jasmine had insisted, her eyes flashing. "The sorceress Thaegan rules there."

"It has always been her stronghold, Jasmine," Barda pointed out patiently. "Yet in the past many travelers passed through it and survived to tell the tale."

"Thaegan is ten times more powerful now than she ever was!" exclaimed Jasmine. "Evil loves evil, and the Shadow Lord has increased her strength so that now she is swollen with vanity as well as wickedness. If we travel through the north we are doomed!"

Lief and Barda glanced at each other. Both had been glad when Jasmine decided to leave the Forests of Silence and join them on their quest to find the lost gems of the Belt of Deltora. It was thanks to her that they had not perished in the Forests. It was thanks to her that the first stone, the golden topaz, was now fixed to the Belt Lief wore hidden under his shirt. They knew that Jasmine's talents would be of great use as they moved on to find the six remaining stones.

But for a long time Jasmine had lived by her wits, with no one to please but herself. She was not used to following the plans of others, and had no fear of speaking her feelings plainly. Now Lief was realizing, with some annoyance, that there were going to be times when Jasmine was an uncomfortable, unruly companion.

"We are sure that one of the gems is hidden at the Lake of Tears, Jasmine," he said sharply. "So we must go there."

Jasmine stamped her foot impatiently. "Of

course!" she exclaimed. "But we do not have to travel all the way through Thaegan's territory to do it. Why are you so stubborn and foolish, Lief? The Lake is at the edge of Thaegan's lands. If we approach it from the south, making a wide circle, we can avoid her notice till the very end."

"Such a journey would force us to cross the Os-Mine Hills, so would take five times as long," growled Barda, before Lief could answer. "And who knows what dangers the Hills themselves might hold? No. I believe we should go the way we have planned."

"I, too," Lief agreed. "So it is two against one."

"It is not!" Jasmine retorted. "Kree and Filli vote with me."

"Kree and Filli do not have a vote," growled Barda, finally losing patience. "Jasmine — come with us or return to the Forests. The decision is yours."

With that, he strode away, with Lief close behind him. Jasmine, after a long minute, walked slowly after them. But she was frowning, and in the days that followed, she had grown more and more grave and silent.

✳

Lief was thinking so deeply that he almost cannoned into Barda, who had stopped abruptly just around a bend in the track. He started to apologize, but Barda waved his arm for silence, and pointed.

They had reached the end of the tree-lined pathway, and directly ahead of them yawned a great chasm, its bare, rocky cliffs gleaming pink in the sunlight. Over the terrible drop swayed a narrow bridge made of rope and wooden planks. And in front of the bridge stood a huge, golden-eyed, dark-skinned man holding a wickedly curved sword.

Like a gaping wound in the earth, the chasm stretched away to left and right as far as the eye could see. Wind blew through it, making a soft, eerie sound, and great brown birds swooped on the gusts like enormous kites, wings spread wide.

There was no way across except the swaying bridge. But the way to the bridge was barred by the golden-eyed giant, who stood unmoving and unblinking, on guard.

2 - Three Questions

Lief stood stiffly, his heart beating fast, as Jasmine followed him around the bend. He heard her take a sharp breath as she, too, saw what was ahead.

The golden-eyed man had noticed them, but he made no move. He just stood, waiting. He wore nothing but a loincloth, yet he did not shiver in the wind. He was so still you could have thought him a statue, except that he breathed.

"He is bewitched," Jasmine whispered, and Kree made a small, moaning sound.

They walked cautiously forward. The man watched them silently. But when finally they stood before him, at the very edge of the terrible drop, he raised his sword warningly.

"We wish to pass, friend," Barda said. "Stand aside."

"You must answer my question," replied the man in a low, rasping voice. "If you answer correctly, you may pass. If you answer wrongly, I must kill you."

"By whose order?" Jasmine demanded.

"By the order of the sorceress Thaegan," rasped the man. At the sound of the name his skin seemed to quiver. "Once, I tried to deceive her, to save a friend from death. Now it is my doom to guard this bridge until truth and lies are one."

He looked from one to the other. "Who will meet my challenge?"

"I will," Jasmine said, shaking off Barda's restraining hand and stepping forward.

The look of fear had disappeared from her face. It had been replaced by an expression that for a moment Lief did not recognize. And then, with amazement, he realized that it was pity.

"Very well." The huge man looked down at his feet. A row of sticks lay there in the dust.

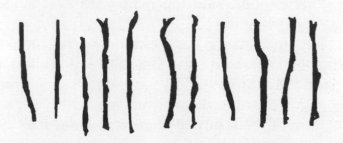

"Change eleven to nine, without removing any sticks," he said harshly.

Lief felt his stomach turn over.

"This is not a fair question," exclaimed Barda. "We are not magicians!"

"The question has been asked," said the man, his golden eyes unblinking. "It must be answered."

Jasmine had been staring at the sticks. Suddenly she crouched and began moving them around. Her body hid what she was doing, but when she stood up again Lief gasped. There were still eleven sticks, but now they read:

"Very good," said the man, with no change of tone. "You may pass."

He stood aside and Jasmine moved onto the bridge. But when Lief and Barda tried to follow her, he barred their way.

"Only the one who answers may cross," he said.

Jasmine had turned and was watching them.

Black wings spread wide, Kree hovered above her head. The bridge swayed dangerously.

"Go on!" Barda called. "We will follow."

Jasmine nodded slightly, turned again, and began walking lightly across the bridge, as carelessly as if it were a tree branch in the Forests of Silence.

"You spoke, so your question is next," said the man with the golden eyes, turning to Barda. "Here it is — what is it that a beggar has, that a rich man needs, and that the dead eat?"

There was silence. Then —

"Nothing," said Barda quietly. "The answer is, 'Nothing.' "

"Very good," said the man. "You may pass."

He stood aside.

"I would like to wait until my companion has answered his question," Barda said, without moving. "Then we can cross the bridge together."

"That is not permitted," said the man. The powerful muscles of his arms tightened slightly on the curved sword.

"Go, Barda," whispered Lief. His skin was tingling with nerves, but he was sure he could answer the question, whatever it was. Jasmine and Barda had succeeded, and he had far more learning than either of them.

Barda frowned, but did not argue further. Lief watched as he stepped onto the bridge and began walking slowly across it, holding tightly to the rails of rope. The rope creaked under his weight. The great birds swooped around him, riding the wind. Far below, there was the thin, snake-like trail of a gleaming river. But Barda did not look down.

"Here is the third question," rasped the man with the golden eyes, stepping back into his place. "It is long, so to be fair I will ask it twice. Listen well."

Lief paid close attention as the man began to speak. The question was in the form of a rhyme:

Thaegan gulps her favorite food
In her cave with all her brood:
Hot, Tot, Jin, Jod,
Fie, Fly, Zan, Zod,
Pik, Snik, Lun, Lod
And the dreaded Ichabod.
Each child holds a slimy toad.
On each toad squirm two fat grubs.
On each grub ride two fleas brave.
How many living in Thaegan's cave?

Lief almost smiled with relief. How many long afternoons had he spent doing sums under the watchful eye of his mother? He could meet this test easily!

He knelt on the ground and as the rhyme was repeated he counted carefully, writing numbers in the dust with his finger.

There were thirteen of Thaegan's children altogether. Plus thirteen toads. Plus twenty-six grubs. Plus fifty-two fleas. That made . . . one hundred and four. Lief checked the sum twice and opened his mouth to speak. Then his heart thudded painfully as, just in time, he realized that he had nearly made a mistake. He had forgotten to add Thaegan herself!

Almost panting at the near disaster, he scrambled to his feet.

"One hundred and five," he gasped.

The man's strange eyes seemed to flash. "You have not answered well," he said. His hand shot out and grabbed Lief's arm with a grip of iron.

Lief gaped at him, feeling the heat of panic rise into his cheeks. "But — the sum is correct!" he stammered. "The children, the toads, the grubs, and the fleas — and Thaegan herself — add up to one hundred and five!"

"Yes," said the man. "But you have forgotten Thaegan's favorite food. A raven, swallowed alive. It was in the cave also, alive in her belly. The answer is one hundred and six."

He lifted his curved sword. "You have not answered well," he repeated. "Prepare to die."

3 ~ Truth and Lies

Lief struggled to free himself. "The question was not fair!" he shouted. "You tricked me! How could I know what Thaegan likes to eat?"

"What you know or do not know is not my concern," said the guardian of the bridge. He raised the sword higher, till its curved blade was level with Lief's neck.

"No!" cried Lief. "Wait!" At this moment of terror, his one thought was for the Belt of Deltora and the topaz fixed to it. If he did nothing to prevent it, this golden-eyed giant would surely find the Belt after he was dead, take it from his body — and perhaps give it to Thaegan. Then Deltora would be lost to the Shadow Lord forever.

I must throw the Belt over the cliff, he thought desperately. I must make sure that Barda and Jasmine see me do it. Then they will have some chance of finding it again. If only I can delay him until I can do it . . .

"You are a trickster and a deceiver!" he cried, slipping his hands under his shirt, feeling for the Belt's fastening. "No wonder you are doomed to guard this bridge until truth and lies are one!"

As he had hoped, the man paused. Anger brightened his golden eyes.

"My suffering was not justly earned," he spat. "It was for pure spite that Thaegan took my freedom and cursed me to be tied to this piece of earth. If you are so interested in truth and lies, we will play another game."

Lief's fingers froze on the Belt. But the flicker of hope that had flared in his heart faded and died with his enemy's next words.

"We will play a game to decide which way you will die," said the man. "You may say one thing, and one thing only. If what you say is true, I will strangle you with my bare hands. If what you say is false, I will cut off your head."

Lief bent his head, pretending to consider, while his fingers secretly struggled with the Belt's catch. The fastening was stiff, and would not open. His hand pressed against the topaz — so hard-won, so soon to be lost, if he did not hurry.

"I am waiting," said the guardian of the bridge. "Make your statement."

True statement, or false? Was it better to be beheaded or strangled? Better to be neither, thought Lief grimly. And then, in a blinding flash, the most wonderful idea came to him.

He looked up boldly at the waiting man. "My head will be cut off," he said clearly.

The man hesitated.

"Well?" cried Lief. "Did you not hear my statement? Is it true or false?"

But he knew that his enemy would have no answer. For if the statement was true, the man was bound to strangle him, thus making it false. And if the statement was false, the man was bound to cut off his head, thus making it true.

And even as he wondered how in his panic he had managed to think of this, the tall figure before him gave a deep, shuddering sigh. Then Lief's eyes widened and he cried out in shock. For the man's flesh had begun rippling, melting — changing shape.

Brown feathers were sprouting from his skin. His legs were shrinking and his feet were spreading, becoming talons. His powerful arms and shoulders were dissolving and re-forming themselves into great wings. His curved sword was becoming a fierce, hooked beak.

And in moments the man was gone, and a huge, proud bird with golden eyes stood on the cliff in his place. With a triumphant cry it spread its wings and soared into the air, joining the other birds swooping and gliding on the wind.

It is my doom to guard this bridge until truth and lies are one.

Lief stared, trembling all over. He could hardly believe what had happened. The guardian of the bridge had been a bird, forced by Thaegan's magic into human form. It had been bound to the earth by her spite as surely as if it had been chained.

And his trick answer had broken Thaegan's spell. He had thought only of saving his own life, but he had broken Thaegan's spell. The bird was free at last.

A sound broke through his racing thoughts. He glanced at the bridge and to his horror saw that it was starting to crumble. Without thinking further, he leapt for it, seizing the rope railings with both hands and running, as he had never imagined he could, over the fearful gap.

He could see Barda and Jasmine standing on the edge of the cliff ahead of him, holding out their arms. He could hear their voices shrieking to him. Behind him, planks rattled together as they slipped from their rope ties and plunged to the river far below.

Soon the rope itself would give way. He knew it. Already it was growing slack. The bridge was sagging, swinging sickeningly as he ran.

All he could think of was to run faster. But he was only halfway across, and he could not run fast enough. Now the planks under his feet were slipping — slipping away! He was stumbling, dropping, the ropes burning his clutching hands. He was dangling in midair, with nowhere to put his feet. And as he hung there, helpless and buffeted by the wind, the planks in front of him — the planks that were his only pathway to safety — began slithering sideways, falling to the river far below.

Painfully, hand over hand, he began swinging himself along the sagging ropes that were all that remained of the bridge, trying not to think of what was below him, what would happen if he lost his grip.

I am playing a game in Del, he told himself feverishly, ignoring the pain of his straining wrists. There is a muddy ditch just below my feet. My friends are watching me, and will laugh at me if I fall. All I have to do is to keep going — hand over hand —

And then he felt a jolt and knew that the ropes had come loose from the cliff-face behind him. Instantly he was swinging forward, hurtling towards the bare, hard face of the cliff in front. In seconds he would slam against it, his bones shattering on the pink rock. He heard his own scream, and the screams of Barda and Jasmine, floating on the wind. He screwed his eyes shut . . .

With a rush something huge swooped under him, and the sickening swing stopped as he felt a warm softness on his face, against his arms. He was being lifted up — up — and the beating of mighty wings was louder in his ears than the wind.

Then he was being clutched by eager hands, and

tumbled onto the dust of solid ground. His ears were ringing. He could hear shouting, laughing voices that seemed very far away. But when he opened his eyes he saw that Jasmine and Barda were leaning over him, and it was they who were shouting, with relief and joy.

He sat up, weak and dizzy, clutching at the ground. His eyes met the golden eyes of the great bird that, but for him, would still be the earthbound guardian of the bridge.

You gave me back my life, the eyes seemed to say. *Now I have returned yours. My debt to you is paid.* Before he could speak, the bird nodded once, spread its wings, and soared away. Lief watched as it joined its companions once more and flew with them, wheeling and shrieking, away along the chasm, into the distance and out of sight.

✳

"You knew that he was a bird," Lief said to Jasmine later, as they moved slowly on. Though he still felt sore and weak, he had refused to rest for long. The very sight of the cliffs made him feel ill. He wanted to get away from them as fast as he could.

Jasmine nodded, glancing at Kree, who was perched on her shoulder with Filli. "I felt it," she said. "And I felt such pity for him when I saw the pain and longing in his eyes."

"In torment he may have been," snorted Barda. "But he would have killed us, without question."

The girl frowned. "He cannot be blamed for that. He was doomed to carry out Thaegan's will. And Thaegan — is a monster."

Her eyes were dark with loathing. And, remembering the riddle that had almost led to his death, Lief thought that now he knew why. He waited until Barda had moved ahead, then spoke to Jasmine again.

"You are not afraid of Thaegan for yourself, but for Kree," he said softly. "Is that not so?"

"Yes," she said, staring straight ahead. "Kree fled to the Forests of Silence after he escaped from her long ago. He was just out of the nest when she took his family. So, in a way, he is like me. I, too, was very young when the Grey Guards took my mother and father."

Her lips tightened. "Kree and I have been together for many years. But I think it is time for us to part. I am leading him into danger. Perhaps to the terrible death he fears more than any other. I cannot bear it."

Kree made a low, trilling sound, and she lifted her arm to him, taking him onto her wrist.

"I know you are willing, Kree," she said. "But I am not. We have talked of this. Now I have truly made up my mind. Please go home to the Forests. If I survive, I will come back for you. If I do not — at least you will be safe."

She stopped, lifted her wrist into the air, and shook it slightly. "Go!" she ordered. "Go home!"

Flapping his wings to steady himself, Kree squawked protestingly.

"Go!" shouted Jasmine. She jerked her hand roughly and Kree was shaken off her wrist. He soared screeching into the air, circled above them once, then flew away.

Jasmine bit her lip and strode on without looking back, Filli chittering miserably on her shoulder.

Lief searched for something comforting to say, but could not find it.

They reached a grove of trees and began following a narrow path that led through the green shade.

"Thaegan hates anything that is beautiful, alive, and free," Jasmine said at last, as they entered a clearing where green ferns clustered and the branches of the trees arched overhead. "The birds say that in the land around the Lake of Tears there was once a town called D'Or — a town like a garden, with golden towers, happy people, and lush flowers and trees. Now it is a dead, sad place."

She waved her hand around her. "As will be all this, when Thaegan and her children have finished their evil work."

Again, there was silence between them, and in the silence they became aware of the rustling of the trees around the clearing.

Jasmine stiffened. "Enemies!" she hissed. "Enemies approach!"

Lief could hear nothing, but by now he knew

better than to ignore one of Jasmine's warnings. The trees here were strange to her, but still she understood their whispering.

He sprinted ahead and caught Barda's arm. Barda stopped and looked around in surprise.

Jasmine's face was pale. "Grey Guards," she whispered. "A whole troop of them. Coming this way."

4 - Rescue

Lief and Barda followed Jasmine up into the trees. After their experience in the Forests of Silence it seemed natural to hide above the ground. They climbed as high as they could, while the sound of tramping feet at last came to their ears. They found a safe, comfortable place to cling as the sound grew louder. Wrapped in Lief's disguising cloak, and further hidden by a thick canopy of leaves, they watched as grey-clad figures began marching into the clearing.

They held themselves very still, flattened against the branches. They thought it would be for only a little time, while the Guards passed. So their hearts sank as they saw the men below them halt, drop their weapons, and throw themselves to the ground.

The troop had chosen the clearing as a resting place it seemed. The three companions exchanged despairing glances. What ill fortune! Now they would have to remain where they were — perhaps for hours.

More and more Guards entered the clearing. Soon it was crowded with grey uniforms and ringing with harsh voices. And then, as the last of the troop came into view, there was the clinking sound of chains to go with the sound of marching boots.

The Guards were escorting a prisoner.

Lief craned his neck to look. The captive looked very different from anyone he had ever seen before. He was very small, with wrinkled blue-grey skin, thin legs and arms, small black eyes like buttons, and a tuft of red hair sticking up from the top of his head. There was a tight leather collar around his neck, with a fastening for a chain or rope dangling from it. He looked exhausted, and the chains that weighed down his wrists and ankles had made raw marks on his skin.

"They have captured a Ralad," breathed Barda, moving to see more clearly.

"What is a Ralad?" asked Lief. He thought he had heard or read the name before, but could not think where.

"The Ralads are a race of builders. They were beloved of Adin and all the kings and queens of Deltora's early times," Barda whispered back. "Their buildings were famous for their strength and cleverness."

Now Lief remembered where he had seen the name — in *The Belt of Deltora*, the little blue book his parents had made him study. He gazed in fascination at the drooping figure below them. "It was the Ralads who built the palace of Del," he murmured. "But he is so small!"

"An ant is tiny," muttered Barda. "Yet an ant can carry twenty times its own weight. It is not size that is important, but heart."

"Be silent!" hissed Jasmine. "The Guards will hear you! As it is, they may catch our scent at any time."

But the Guards had plainly walked a long way, and were tired. They were interested in nothing but the food and drink now being unpacked from baskets the leaders had placed in the middle of the clearing.

Two of them pushed the prisoner roughly to the ground at the side of the clearing and threw him a bottle of water. Then they turned their attention to their meal.

Jasmine stared with disgust as the guards tore at their food and splashed drink into their mouths so that it ran down their chins and spilt on the ground.

But Lief was watching the Ralad man, whose eyes were fixed on the scraps of food that were being scattered on the grass of the clearing. Clearly, he was starving.

"The scrag is hungry!" sniggered one of the Guards, pointing a half-gnawed bone in the Ralad man's direction. "Here, scrag!"

He crawled across to where the prisoner was sitting and held out the bone. The starving man cringed, then, unable to resist the food, leaned forward. The Guard hit him hard on the nose with the bone and snatched it away. The other Guards roared with laughter.

"Beasts!" hissed Jasmine, completely forgetting, in her anger, her own warning about being heard.

"Be still," whispered Barda grimly. "There are too many of them. There is nothing we can do. Yet."

The Guards ate and drank till they could eat and drink no more. Then, sprawled carelessly together like a mass of grey grubs, they lay back, closed their eyes, and began to snore.

As quietly as they could, the three companions climbed from branch to branch until they were directly above the Ralad prisoner. He was sitting perfectly still, his shoulders hunched and his head bowed.

Was he, too, asleep? They knew they could not risk startling him awake. If he cried out, all was lost.

Jasmine dug into her pocket and brought out a stem of dried berries. Carefully she leaned out from the tree and threw the stem so that it fell just in front of the motionless captive.

They heard him take a sharp breath. He looked up to the clear sky above where the stem lay, but, of course, saw nothing. His long grey fingers stretched out cautiously and grabbed the prize. He glanced around to make sure that this was not another

Guards' cruel joke, then crushed the stem to his mouth and began tearing at the berries ravenously.

His chains clinked faintly, but the snoring figures around him did not stir.

"Very well," Jasmine breathed. Taking careful aim, she dropped another stem of berries squarely into the prisoner's lap. This time he looked straight up, and his button eyes widened with shock as he saw the three faces looking down at him.

Lief, Barda, and Jasmine quickly pressed their fingers to their lips, warning him to be silent. He did not make a sound and crammed berries into his mouth as he watched the strangers edging carefully down the tree towards him.

They already knew that they had no chance of freeing him from his chains without waking the Guards. They had another plan. It was dangerous, but it would have to do. Jasmine and Lief had refused to leave the prisoner to the mercy of his captors, and Barda had not needed much persuading. He was the only one of them who knew of the Ralad people, and the thought of one being held prisoner by the Grey Guards was horrible to him.

While Jasmine kept watch from the tree, Lief and Barda slipped to the ground beside the little man and made signs to him not to fear. Trembling, the prisoner nodded. Then he did something surprising. With the tip of one thin finger he made a strange mark upon the ground and looked up at them inquiringly.

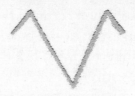

Baffled, Lief and Barda glanced at one another, and then back to him. He saw that they did not understand his meaning. His black eyes grew fearful and he quickly brushed the mark away. But still he seemed to trust the newcomers — or perhaps he thought that no situation could be worse than the one he was in. As the Guards slept on, snoring like beasts, he allowed himself to be quickly and quietly wrapped in Lief's cloak.

They had decided that their only hope was to carry him away, chains and all. They hoped that the tightly wrapped cloak would stop the chains from clinking together, alerting his enemies.

The chains made the little man heavier than he would otherwise have been, but Barda had no difficulty in picking him up and putting him over one shoulder. They knew that to return to the trees, carrying such a burden, would be clumsy and dangerous. But the prisoner had been lying very near the mouth of the path. All they had to do was reach it and creep silently away.

It was a risk they were all prepared to take. And all would have been well if one of the Guards, dreaming, perhaps, had not, right at that moment, rolled over and flung out his arm, hitting his neighbor on the chin.

The Guard who had been struck woke with a roar, looked wildly around to see who had hit him, and caught sight of Lief and Barda running away down the path.

He shouted the alarm. In seconds, the clearing was alive with angry Guards, roused from their sleep and furious to find their prisoner gone.

5 ~ Terror

Howling like beasts, the Guards thundered down the path after Lief and Barda. All of them carried slings and a supply of the poisonous bubbles they called "blisters." All were fitting blisters to their slings as they ran. They knew that as soon as they had clear aim and could hurl the blisters, the running figures ahead of them would fall, helpless and screaming in pain.

Lief and Barda knew it, too. And so, perhaps, did the Ralad man, for he moaned in despair as he bumped on Barda's shoulder. But the path was winding, so there was no clear aim, and fear gave Lief and Barda's feet wings. They were staying well ahead.

But Lief knew this could not last. Already, he was panting. Weakened from his ordeal in the chasm, he did not have the strength he needed to outrun the enemy. Grey Guards could run for days and nights without rest, and could smell out their prey wherever it was hiding.

Far behind he heard thumping, clattering sounds and the angry shouts of falling men. With a thrill of gratitude, he guessed that Jasmine had been following through the trees, dropping dead branches across the path to trip and delay their pursuers.

Be careful, Jasmine, he thought. Do not let them see you.

Jasmine could have remained hidden and safe with Filli. The Guards would never have known that there had been three strangers in the clearing, not just two. But it was not her way to see friends in trouble and do nothing.

With a start, Lief saw her leap lightly to the ground just ahead. He had not realized how close to them she was.

"I have set them an obstacle course," she said gleefully, as they reached her. "Thorny vine twined round dead branches in six places along the path. That will slow them down!" Her eyes were sparkling with pleasure.

"Keep moving!" grunted Barda. "Their anger will only make them run faster!"

They rounded a bend and to his horror Lief saw that ahead was a long stretch of path with no curves at all. It seemed to go on and on, straight as an arrow, vanishing into the distance.

The Guards could not ask for clearer aim than this. As soon as they reached this spot, the blisters would start flying, for they would see their enemies clearly, however far ahead they were. Lief's heart pounded in his aching chest as he fought down despair.

"Off to the side!" hissed Barda, abruptly swerving from the path. "It is our only chance!"

The trees here were slender, with delicate trailing branches — useless for climbing. A carpet of springy grass spread between them, and wild sweetplum bushes were dotted here and there, plump, purple fruits glistening among fresh green leaves.

Lief had never seen sweetplums growing wild before. He had a sudden vision of how pleasant it would have been to wander here peacefully, picking the rich-smelling fruit and eating it straight from the bush. That, no doubt, was what he, Barda, and Jasmine would have done — if they had not met the troop of Guards and their prisoner on the way.

But they *had* met the Guards, and the prisoner. So instead of enjoying the afternoon, they were running for their lives.

Lief glanced at the bundle bobbing on Barda's shoulder. The Ralad man was no longer groaning, and there was no movement within the folds of the cloak. Perhaps he had fainted. Perhaps he was dead of starvation and terror, and all this had been for nothing.

Abruptly, the ground began to slope away, and Lief saw that their steps were taking them into a little valley that had not been visible from the path. Here the sweetplum bushes were larger, and growing more thickly. The air was filled with their rich perfume.

Jasmine sniffed as she ran. "This is a perfect place to hide!" she muttered excitedly. "The smell of these fruits will mask our scent."

Lief glanced behind him. Already the grass bent by their running feet had sprung back into place. There was no sign of the way they had taken. For the first time since they left the path he felt a flicker of hope.

He followed Barda and Jasmine to the bottom of the valley. They pushed into the midst of the bushes, which rose above their heads, hiding them completely. In silence, they crept through the dim, green shade. The ground was damp underfoot, and somewhere there was the gurgling of running water. Sweetplums hung everywhere like tiny, glowing lanterns.

They had been under cover for only a few minutes when Jasmine stopped and raised her hand warningly. "I hear them," she breathed. "They are nearing the place where we left the path."

Crouching very still, listening carefully, Lief finally heard what her sharper ears had heard before him — the sound of running feet. The sound became louder, louder — and then the feet faltered. The first of the Guards had come to the straight section of the path. Lief imagined the leaders peering ahead and seeing no one.

There was a moment's silence. He held his breath at the thought of them sniffing the air, muttering to each other. There was a loud, harsh sound that could have been a laugh or a curse. And then, to his overwhelming relief and joy, he heard an order barked, and the sound of the whole troop turning. In seconds the Guards were marching back the way they had come.

"They have given up," he breathed. "They think we have outrun them."

"It may be a trap," Barda muttered grimly.

The sound of marching feet gradually faded away and though the three companions waited, motionless, for several long minutes, nothing disturbed the silence. Finally, at a whisper from Jasmine, Filli skittered away to the nearest tree and ran up the trunk. In moments he was back, chattering softly.

"All is well," Jasmine said, standing up and stretching. "Filli cannot see them. They have truly gone."

Lief stood up beside her, easing his cramped muscles with relief. He pulled a sweetplum from the bush beside him and bit into it, sighing with pleasure as the sweet, delicious juice cooled his parched throat.

"There are better fruits further along," said Jasmine, pointing ahead.

"First I must see how my poor piece of baggage is faring," said Barda. He unwrapped the cloak and was soon cradling the Ralad man in his arms.

"Is he dead?" asked Lief quietly.

Barda shook his head. "He is unconscious — and no wonder. The Ralad are a strong people, but no one can resist starvation, exhaustion, and fear forever. Who knows how long our friend has been a prisoner of the Guards, or how far he has walked in heavy chains without being given any food or rest?"

Lief looked at the small man curiously. "I have never seen anyone like him before," he said. "What was that sign he drew upon the ground?"

"I do not know. When he awakes, we will ask him." Barda groaned as he lifted the Ralad man up again. "He has caused us some trouble, but still the meeting was fortunate," he added. "He can guide us from here. The village of Raladin, where he comes from, is very near the Lake of Tears. Let us find a place where we can sit in more comfort and remove these chains."

They pushed on through the bushes. The further they moved into the little valley, the more enchanting it seemed. Soft moss covered the ground like a thick green carpet and nodding flowers clustered everywhere. Brightly colored butterflies fluttered around the sweetplum bushes, and the sun, filtering through the delicate leaves of the slender trees, shed a gentle, green-gold light over everything it touched.

Never had Lief seen such beauty. He could tell from Barda's face that he felt the same. Even Jasmine was soon looking around with warm pleasure.

They reached a small clearing and gratefully sank down onto the moss. There Barda used Jasmine's dagger to cut the tight leather collar from the Ralad man's neck and break the locks on his chains. As he pulled the chains away he frowned at the rubbed, raw patches on the man's wrists and ankles.

"They are not so bad." Jasmine inspected the wounds casually. She pulled a small jar from her pocket and unscrewed the lid. "This is of my own making, from my mother's recipe," she said, lightly spreading a pale green cream onto the raw places. "It heals skin quickly. It was often useful . . . in the Forests of Silence."

Lief glanced at her. She was looking down, frowning fiercely as she screwed the lid back on the jar.

She is homesick, Lief thought suddenly. She misses Kree, and the Forests, and the life she had there. Just as I miss my home, and my friends, and my mother and father.

Not for the first time he felt a stab in his heart as he thought of all he had left behind in Del. He thought of his room — tiny, but safe and full of his own treasures. He thought of evenings in front of the fire. Running wild in the streets with his friends. Even working with his father at the forge.

Suddenly he longed for a hot, home-cooked meal. He longed for a warm bed and a comforting voice bidding him good night.

He jumped up, furious with himself. How could he be so weak, so childish? "I am going to explore," he said loudly. "I will collect some sweetplums for us to eat, and wood for a fire."

He did not wait for an answer from Barda and Jasmine, but strode to the edge of the clearing and through a gap between two trees.

The sweetplum bushes here were even more heavily laden than the ones he had already seen. He walked between them, using his cloak as a pouch to hold the fragrant fruits he picked. There were few dead sticks, but those there were he collected. Even a small fire would be welcome when night came.

His eyes fixed to the ground, he walked on. At last he stumbled on a good piece of flat wood, far bigger than anything else he had seen. It was damp, and moss had grown over it, but he knew it would soon dry and burn once the fire was well alight.

Pleased, he picked it up and, straightening his back, looked around to see where he was. And it was then that he saw something very surprising, right in front of his nose. It was a sign — old, broken, and battered, but plainly made by human hands:

RING
AND
ENTER

Beside the sign, hanging from a tree branch, was a metal bell.

How strange, Lief thought. He peered through the bushes beyond the sign and jumped with surprise. Directly ahead was a strip of smooth, bright green lawn. And beyond the lawn, in the distance, was what looked like a small white house. Smoke was drifting from the chimney.

"Barda!" he cried, his voice cracking. "Jasmine!"

He heard them exclaiming and running towards him, but he could not tear his eyes away from the little house. As they reached him, he pointed and they gasped in amazement.

"I never thought to find people living here!" exclaimed Barda. "What a piece of good fortune!"

"A bath!" cried Lief happily. "Hot food! And perhaps a bed for the night!"

" 'Ring and Enter,' " said Jasmine, reading the sign. "Very well, then. Let us obey!"

Lief stretched out his hand and rang the bell. It made a cheery, welcoming sound, and together the friends ran through the bushes and onto the green lawn.

They had taken only a few steps before they realized that something was terribly wrong. Desperately they tried to turn back. But it was too late. Already they were sinking — to their knees . . . their thighs . . . their waists . . .

Beneath the green-covered surface of what they had thought was a fine flat lawn — was quicksand.

6 - Nij and Doj

Floundering, terrified, they screamed for help as the quicksand sucked them down. Already they had sunk nearly to their chests. Soon — soon they would disappear under the treacherous green surface that they now knew was simply a thin layer of some slimy water plant.

The fruit and sticks that Lief had been carrying had scattered and sunk without trace, but the big piece of wood he had found was still lying on the surface of the quicksand between the three struggling friends. It floats because it is flat and wide, Lief thought through his panic. It is floating where nothing else will.

There was a shout, and he saw, hurrying from the little white cottage, two plump, grey-haired figures carrying a long pole between them. Help was coming. But by the time it arrived it would be too late. Too late. Unless . . .

Lief reached out for the flat piece of wood and just managed to touch its edge with the tips of his fingers.

"Jasmine! Barda!" he shouted. "Hold on to this wood. At the edges. Gently. Try to — to stretch out and spread yourselves flat, as though you were swimming."

They heard him. They did as he asked. In moments the three companions were spread out around the piece of wood like the petals of a giant flower or the spokes of a wheel. High on Jasmine's shoulder, Filli chattered with fear, clutching her hair with his tiny hands.

They were no longer sinking. The wood was holding them almost steady. But for how long could their balance last? If one of them panicked — if the wood tipped one way or the other, it would slide under the quicksand and they would go with it and be lost.

"Help is coming!" gasped Lief. "Hold on!"

He did not dare to raise his head to look for the two old people in case the movement disturbed his balance. But he could hear their gasping cries. They were very close now.

Oh, quickly, he begged them in his mind. Please hurry!

He heard them reach the edge of the quicksand. He could not understand their words, because they were speaking in a strange tongue. But their voices were urgent. It was clear that they wanted to help.

"Taem hserf!" the man was panting.

"Knis ti tel ton od!" the woman exclaimed in answer. *"Tou ti teg!"*

There was a splash. The quicksand surged and rippled. Lief clutched at his piece of wood and cried out. Green slime and sand covered his mouth, his nose . . . Then he felt something catch him around the back, curving under his arms, holding him up, pulling him forward.

Choking and spluttering, he opened his eyes. Whatever was holding him — a large metal hook, perhaps — was attached to the end of a long wooden pole. Jasmine and Barda had caught hold of the pole itself. Like him, they were being towed slowly towards firm ground by the two old people who heaved together, grunting with the effort.

There was nothing the three friends could do to help themselves. Progress was agonizingly slow. The quicksand sucked at their bodies, holding them back. But the two old people would not give up. Red-faced, they sweated and puffed, pulling at the pole with all their might.

And at last, Lief saw Jasmine and Barda pulled out of the sand's grip. With a horrible, sucking sound it released them and they flopped together onto dry land — wet, filthy, and covered in slime.

Moments later it was his turn. His body popped from the ooze and onto the bank like a cork from a bottle — so suddenly that the two old people tumbled backwards and sat down hard. They gasped, clutching each other and laughing.

Lief lay, panting on the ground, gabbling his relief and thanks. Hard against his back was the hook that had saved his life, but he did not care. He found that he was still clutching the piece of wood, and laughed. Rough and rubbishy as it was, it, too, had played its part. He was glad it had not been lost in the sand. He sat up and looked around.

The two old people were picking themselves up, chattering excitedly to one another.

"Efas era yeht!" cried the old woman.

"Egamad on!" her companion agreed.

"What are they talking about?" muttered Jasmine. "I cannot understand a word they say."

Lief glanced at her. Her face was thunderous.

"Do not frown at them so, Jasmine," he whispered urgently. "They saved our lives!"

"They nearly *took* our lives, with their foolish 'Ring and Enter' sign," she snapped. "I do not see why I should be grateful to them!"

"They may not have put the sign there," Barda pointed out calmly. "It may have been here longer than they have. It looked very old — broken and battered."

Suddenly, Lief had a terrible thought. He looked down at the piece of wood he held in his hand. It, too, looked very old. And it, too, had a jagged edge, as though it had been broken away from something larger, a long time ago.

Slowly he rubbed away the moss that still clung to one side. His face began to burn as faded words and letters became visible.

In his mind's eye he fitted this piece of wood to the sign on the other side of the quicksand.

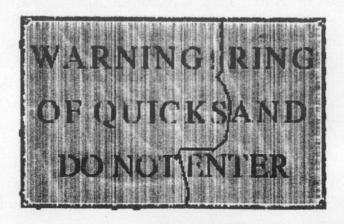

Silently, he held up the piece of wood so that Jasmine and Barda could see the words. Their eyes widened and they groaned as they realized how they had made the mistake that had nearly been their death.

The two old people were bustling up to them. When they in their turn saw the piece of broken sign, they exclaimed and looked shocked.

"*Ti was yeht!*" cried the woman.

"*Ti wonk ton did yeht. Sloof!*" growled the man. He took the piece of sign from Lief's hand and shook his head. Then he pointed across to the other side of the quicksand and made breaking movements with his hands.

Lief nodded. "Yes, the warning sign was broken," he said, though he knew they could not understand him. "We were fools for not realizing that, and for rushing forward as we did."

"The sign has been broken for years!" muttered Jasmine, still angry. "The piece that has fallen off is covered in moss. They must have known. And why is there a bell hanging from the tree?"

"If a ring of quicksand surrounds their land, perhaps they rarely leave it," Barda murmured. "If that is so, how could they know what is beyond?"

The old woman smiled at Lief. Her smile was sweet and merry. She was pink-cheeked, with twinkling blue eyes, and she was wearing a long blue dress. Her apron was white and her grey hair was tied in a knot on the back of her neck.

Lief smiled back at her. She reminded him of a picture in one of the old storybooks in the bookshelf at home. It made him feel warm and safe just looking at her. The old man was also comforting to look at. He had a kind, cheery face, a fringe of grey hair around a bald patch on his head, and a bushy white mustache.

"*Nij,*" the woman said, patting her chest and bowing slightly. Then she pulled the old man forward. "*Doj,*" she said, tapping him.

Lief realized that she was telling him their names. "Lief," he said in return, pointing at himself. Then he held out his hand to Jasmine and Barda and said their names as well.

With each introduction, Nij and Doj bowed and smiled. Then they pointed to the little white house, mimed washing and drinking, and looked at the three companions questioningly.

"Certainly," beamed Barda, nodding vigorously. "Thank you. You are kind."

"*Yrgnuh era ew,*" said Doj, patting him on the back. He and Nij both roared with laughter as if at some great joke, and began walking together towards the house.

"Are you forgetting the Ralad man?" asked Jasmine in a low voice, as the three companions followed. "He will wake and find us gone. He may look for us. What if he falls into the quicksand, too?"

Barda shrugged. "I doubt that he will try to find us," he said comfortably. "He will be too eager to make his way home again. Though Ralads have always traveled to do their building work, they hate to be away from Raladin for too long."

As the girl lingered, looking back over her shoulder, his voice sharpened. "Come along, Jasmine!" he complained. "Anyone would think that you enjoyed being wet and covered in slime!"

Lief was hardly listening. His feet were quickening as he approached the little white house with the smoking chimney and the flower gardens. *Home*, his heart was telling him. *Friends. Here you can rest. Here you will be safe.*

Barda strode beside him, as eager as Lief was to reach the welcoming house and to enjoy the comforts inside.

Jasmine trailed behind, with Filli nestled against her hair. She was still frowning. If either Lief or Barda had paid attention to her, had listened to her doubts and suspicions, they might have slowed their steps.

But neither of them did. And they did not realize their mistake until long after the green door had shut behind them.

7 - Shocks

Nij and Doj led the three companions into a large, bright kitchen with a stone floor. Polished pots and pans hung from hooks above the big fuel stove and a large table stood in the center of the room. It reminded Lief of the kitchen in the forge, and he would have been happy to stay there — especially as, like Barda and Jasmine, he was wet and muddy.

But Nij and Doj seemed shocked at the idea of their guests sitting in the kitchen, and bustled them into a cosy sitting room beyond. Here an open fire burned, and there were comfortable-looking easy chairs and a woven carpet on the floor.

With many nods and smiles, Nij gave Jasmine, Lief, and Barda rugs to wrap themselves in, and made them sit by the fire. Then she and Doj rushed away again, making signs to say they would return.

Soon Lief could hear clattering and murmuring in the kitchen. He guessed that the two old people were heating water for baths and perhaps preparing a meal. *"Retaw liob,"* Nij was saying busily. And Doj was laughing as he worked. *"Noos taem hserf! Noos taem hserf!"* he was chanting in a singsong voice.

Lief's heart warmed. Whatever these people had, they would give to help the strangers in trouble.

"They are very kind," he said lazily. He felt relaxed for the first time in days. The fire was cheery, and the rug around his shoulders was comforting. The room, too, made him feel at home. There was a jug of yellow daisies on the mantelpiece — daisies exactly like the ones that grew wild by the forge gate. Over the fireplace hung a framed piece of embroidery, no doubt made by Nij's own hands.

"Yes, they are very good," murmured Barda. "It is for people such as these that we wish to save Deltora."

Jasmine sniffed. Lief glanced at her and wondered at the restless look on her face. Then he realized that, of course, she had never been inside a house like this, never met ordinary people like Nij and Doj before. She had spent her life in the Forests, among trees, under the sky. No wonder she felt uncomfortable here, instead of at peace as he and Barda did.

Filli was hunched on Jasmine's shoulder with his paws over his eyes. He was not happy, either, though Nij and Doj had made him welcome, smiling and trying to stroke him.

"Lief," Jasmine whispered, as she saw him looking at her. "Is the Belt safe? Is the topaz still in place?"

Lief realized with a small shock that he had forgotten all about the Belt until this moment. He felt for it, and was relieved to find that it was still securely fixed around his waist.

He lifted up his filthy shirt to look at it. Its steel links were clogged with mud and slime. The topaz was thickly coated, its golden lights hidden. With his fingers he began to clean the gem of the worst of the murky grime. It seemed wrong that it should be so fouled.

His work stopped abruptly as Doj hurried in from the kitchen, carrying a tray. Lief cursed his own carelessness. The rug which was wrapped around him hid the Belt from the doorway, but this was just a fortunate chance. Nij and Doj were kind and good, but it was vital that the quest for the Belt of Deltora was revealed to as few people as possible. He should have taken more care.

He sat perfectly still, his head bent and his hands clasped over the topaz, while Doj set down the tray, which was loaded with drinks and a plate of small cakes.

"Here, scum!" said Doj. *"Enjoy your last meal on earth."*

Lief's scalp prickled with shock. Was he hearing things? Was he dreaming? He stole a look at Barda and saw that he was smiling pleasantly. Jasmine, too, seemed undisturbed.

He felt a nudge on his arm and looked up. Doj was smiling at him, handing him a cup of what looked like sweetplum juice. But with a thrill of horror Lief saw that the old man's face was horribly changed. The skin was mottled and covered in lumps and sores. The eyes were yellow, flat, and cold, like snake's eyes, over a nose that was just two flaring black holes. The grinning mouth was greedy and cruel, with crooked metal spikes for teeth and a fat blue tongue that crept out and licked at swollen lips.

Lief shrieked aloud and cowered back.

"Lief, what is the matter?" cried Jasmine, alarmed.

"What are you thinking of?" growled Barda at the same moment, glancing in an embarrassed way at the horrible monster who was still holding out the cup.

The blood was pounding in Lief's head. He could hardly breathe, but his mind was racing.

Plainly, his friends were not seeing what he was seeing. To them, Doj was still the kindly old man that Lief had once believed him to be.

But that vision had been a lie — an illusion, created by some evil magic. Lief knew that now. He also knew that at all costs the hideous being must not find out that for him, at least, the spell had been broken.

He clutched at the topaz beneath his shirt and forced himself to smile and nod. "I — was dozing," he stammered. "I — woke with a shock. I am sorry." He mimed sleeping and waking suddenly, and pretended to laugh at himself.

Doj laughed, too. And it was horrible to see his bared, shining teeth, and his dripping mouth gaping wide.

He handed the cup to Lief and walked back towards the kitchen. *"Reverof peels nac uoy noos,"* he said, at the door. Again he licked his lips. And again Lief heard the words for what they really were: *"Soon you can sleep forever."*

The words were not a strange language, but ordinary words turned backwards! His head whirling, phrases and comments coming back to him, Lief saw that every sentence Doj and Nij had said had been turned backwards.

In a daze of horror he watched Doj leave the room. He heard him begin clattering round in the kitchen with Nij, raising his voice in the same sing-song chant: *"Noos taem hserf, noos taem hserf!"*

"Fresh meat soon, fresh meat soon!"

Lief's whole body shuddered as if blasted by an icy wind. He swung round to Jasmine and Barda, and as he did he saw the living room as it really was.

It was a grim, dark cell. The walls were stone, dripping with greasy water. The soft carpet was made of the skins of small animals, roughly sewn together. But the embroidery over the mantelpiece was still complete. For the first time he stared at it with clear eyes:

"Lief, what is the matter?"

He tore his eyes away from the terrible words and looked at Jasmine. She was watching him in puzzlement, a cup halfway to her lips.

"Do — do not drink that!" Lief managed to say.

Jasmine frowned. "I am thirsty!" she protested, and lifted the cup.

Desperately, Lief struck it from her hand and it fell to the floor. Jasmine sprang up with a cry of anger.

"Be still!" he hissed. "You do not understand. There is danger here. The drink — who knows what is in it!"

"Are you mad, Lief?" yawned Barda. "It is delicious!" He was leaning back on the stinking animal skins. His eyes were partly closed.

Lief shook his arm frantically, realizing with a sinking heart that the big man had already drunk half of his drink. "Barda, get up!" he begged. "They are trying to drug us! Already you feel the drug's effects."

"Nonsense," drawled Barda. "Never have I seen such kindly people as Nij and Doj. Are they husband and wife, do you think, or brother and sister?"

Nij. Doj . . . Suddenly the names turned themselves around in Lief's head and he saw them, too, for what they really were.

"They are brother and sister," he said grimly. "Their names are not Nij and Doj, but Jin and Jod. They are two of the sorceress Thaegan's children. They were named in that rhyme the guardian of the bridge repeated to me. They are monsters! When we are asleep they will kill us — and then eat us!"

"That is a poor joke, Lief," Jasmine frowned.

And Barda just blinked in concern. He looked around the room, and Lief knew that all he was seeing was homely comfort. Barda's own eyes were telling him that fear had turned his companion's wits.

"Noos taem hserf, noos taem hserf!" chanted the monster Jod in the kitchen. And his sister joined in, her voice raised over the sound of a sharpening knife. *"Wets ylevol! Wets ylevol!"*

Barda smiled sleepily. "Hear how they sing at

their work?" he said, leaning over and patting Lief's arm. "How could you think they were anything other than what they seem? Rest, now. You will be feeling better soon."

Lief shook his head desperately. What was he going to do?

8 - Eyes Wide Open

L ief knew that he had to break the spell that was
blinding Barda and Jasmine.

But how was he to do it? He did not understand how he himself had come to understand the
truth. It had happened so suddenly. He had been
cleaning the topaz when Doj came in and —

The topaz!

Some half-remembered sentences from his fa-
ther's little blue book, *The Belt of Deltora*, drifted into
his head.

He closed his eyes, concentrating hard, till he
saw the page of the book in his mind.

✝ **The topaz is a powerful gem, and its strength
increases as the moon grows full. The topaz protects its
wearer from the terrors of the night. It has the power to**

open doors into the spirit world. It strengthens and clears the mind . . .

It strengthens and clears the mind!

Lief grasped the topaz tightly as his thoughts raced. He remembered that his hand had been on the topaz when he managed to meet the last test set by the guardian of the bridge. He had been cleaning the topaz when he realized Doj was not what he seemed.

The golden gem was the key!

Without bothering to explain, he grabbed Barda's hand, and Jasmine's, and pulled them forward until they touched the topaz.

Their gasps of astonishment and annoyance changed almost instantly to smothered shrieks of horror. Their eyes bulged as they looked around the room — saw, at last, what Lief was seeing, and heard the words floating from the kitchen.

"Fresh meat soon! Fresh meat soon!"

"Lovely stew! Lovely stew!"

"I did not like them, or their house," hissed Jasmine. "And Filli felt the same. But I thought it was because we had grown up in the Forests, and did not know how people in the world behaved."

"I — " Barda swallowed, and brushed his hand over his forehead. "How could I have been so blind?"

"We were all blinded by magic," Lief whispered.

"But the topaz has strengthened and cleared our minds so that we can resist the spell."

Barda shook his head. "I thought it was strange that the Grey Guards did not search for us after they lost sight of us on the trail," he muttered. "Now I understand it. They must have guessed where we were hiding. They knew we would at last wander to the quicksand and be caught by Jin and Jod. No wonder they laughed as they went away."

"Jin and Jod are clumsy and slow," said Lief. "If they were not, they would not need magic or a sleeping drug to catch their victims. We have a chance . . ."

"If we can find a way out." Jasmine darted away and began searching the walls of the cell, running her fingers over the dripping stones.

Barda staggered to his feet and tried to follow, but stumbled and caught Lief's arm to steady himself. The big man was swaying and very pale.

"It is their accursed drink," he mumbled. "I did not take enough to put me to sleep, but it has weakened me, I fear."

They heard Jasmine hissing their names. She was beckoning from the other side of the room. As quickly as they could, Barda and Lief hurried over to her.

She had found a door. It had been made to look like part of the wall. Only a narrow crack showed its outline. Filled with frantic hope, they pushed their fingers into the crack and tugged.

The door swung open without noise. They looked beyond it, and their hopes died.

The door did not lead to a way out, but to a storeroom piled to the roof with a tangled mass of possessions. There were clothes of every size and type, musty and stained with damp. There were rusted pieces of armor, helmets, and shields. There were swords and daggers, dull with neglect and cluttered together in a towering pile. There were two chests overflowing with jewels, and two more heaped with gold and silver coins.

The three companions stared in horror, realizing that these were the possessions of all the travelers trapped and killed by Jin and Jod in the past. No weapon had been strong enough, no fighter clever enough, to defeat them.

"The broken sign has lured many into the quicksand," breathed Jasmine.

Lief nodded grimly. "It is a neat trap. The monsters hear the bell ring, and run down to pull out whoever has fallen in. Their victims are grateful, and also see only what Jin and Jod want them to see. So they do not fight them, but come tamely up to the house . . ."

"To be drugged, killed, and eaten," said Barda, gritting his teeth. "As nearly happened to us."

"And as still might," Jasmine reminded him, "if we do not find a way out of here!"

And at that moment, they heard the faint clanging of the bell. Someone else had read the broken sign. Someone else was about to be caught in the quicksand trap.

For a single moment they stood, frozen. Then Lief's mind began to work again. "Back to the fireplace!" he hissed. "Lie down! Pretend to be — "

He did not have to finish. His companions understood and were already hurrying back to their places, emptying the drugged juice from their cups and throwing themselves down on the floor.

"Doj, team erom!" they heard Jin screech from the kitchen. *"Kooh eht teg!"*

"Tsaef a!" gibbered her brother excitedly. *"Tey peelsa srehto eht era?"* There was the clatter of a lid being thrown back on a pot and the sound of running footsteps.

Like Jasmine and Barda, Lief was pretending to be unconscious when Jin came in to check on them. He did not stir when he felt her foot nudge him. But as she grunted with satisfaction and moved away he opened his eyes to slits and looked at her through his eyelashes.

She had turned and was lumbering quickly towards the door. He could only see a humped mass of sickly green-white flesh covered in black bristles, and the back of a bald head from which sprouted three stubby horns. He could not see her face, but of that he was very glad.

"Efink eht rof ydaer era yeht!" she bellowed as she left the cell, slamming the door after her. Shuddering, Lief heard her footsteps in the kitchen and the sound of another slamming door. Then there was silence. She and her brother had both left the house.

"So we are ready for the knife, are we? And now they have caught another poor wretch in their trap!" muttered Barda, clambering unsteadily to his feet and hurrying to the door with the others.

"It must be the Ralad man," hissed Jasmine. She ran into the kitchen, with the others close behind.

Now that the spell had been broken, they saw the kitchen with new eyes. It was dark, stinking, and filthy. The stone floor was caked with ancient grime. Old bones lay scattered everywhere. In the darkest corner there was a small bed of moldy straw. By the look of the frayed rope attached to a ring on the wall above it, some sort of pet had slept there until quite recently, when it had chewed its way to freedom.

The companions only glanced at all these things. Their attention was fixed on the great pot of water bubbling under its lid on the stove, the huge pile of roughly sliced onions, and the two long, sharpened knives lying ready on the greasy table.

Lief stared, his stomach churning. Then he jumped as his ears, sharpened by fear, picked up a small, stealthy sound from deep within the house. Someone — or something — was moving.

His companions had heard it, too. "Out!" hissed Barda. "Make haste!"

They crept into the open, gasping with relief as finally they were able to breathe in fresh, clean air. They looked around cautiously.

The sweet little cottage they thought they had seen was in fact a grim, hulking square of white stones with no windows. The flower gardens were nothing but beds of onions and thistles. Rough grass stretched on all sides, leading always to the bright green band that marked the quicksand.

In the distance, they could see Jin and Jod. Shouting angrily at one another, they were digging their long pole into a patch of quicksand where something had fallen in, disturbing the green slime before sinking out of sight.

A wave of sadness swept over Lief.

"They were not in time to save him. He has gone under," said Barda, his face showing his pain.

"Very well, then," snapped Jasmine. "We have nothing to stay for. So why are we standing here, when at any moment they could turn and see us?"

Lief glanced at her. She returned his gaze defiantly, her lips pressed tightly together and her chin raised. Then she turned and began walking quickly around the house, out of sight.

Lief helped Barda to follow her.

The back of the house was just the same as the front, with a single door and no windows. On all sides, bare grass stretched away, ending in the same band of bright green. Beyond, there was forest. But the quicksand circled the whole of Jin and Jod's domain like a moat.

"There must be a way across!" muttered Lief. "I cannot believe that they never leave this place."

Jasmine was scanning the green band with narrowed eyes. Suddenly, she pointed to a slightly mottled-looking section almost opposite the house. The place was marked by a huge rock on the bank. "There!" she exclaimed, and began running.

9 - Stepping Stones

As quickly as he could, with Barda leaning on his shoulder, Lief hurried after Jasmine. When finally they reached her, she was standing beside the rock at the edge of the quicksand. Now Lief could see what had made the green slime look mottled in this spot. In the middle of the moat floated a cluster of pale green leaves marked with red — the leaves of some swamp plant, perhaps.

The edges of the leaves were straight, so that where they touched they fitted together like a puzzle. Where there were gaps between them, the bright green of the quicksand slime showed ominously.

Lief looked more closely and realized that the red markings on the leaves were even stranger than they had first appeared. They were numbers, letters, and symbols.

He clutched Jasmine's arm.

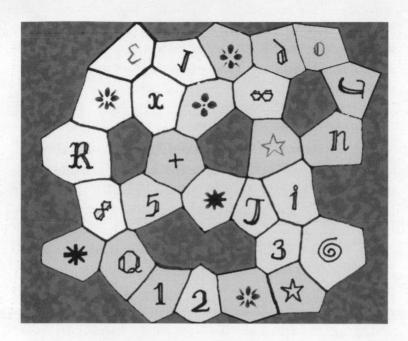

"There is a pathway hidden here, I am sure of it!" he whispered in excitement. "There are stepping stones under some of those leaves."

"But which ones?" muttered Jasmine. "We would have to be very sure. The cluster is in the middle of the quicksand. We have nothing long enough to test which leaves are solid and which are not. We would have to leap, and trust that there is no mistake."

"The topaz, Lief," Barda urged. "Perhaps it will help you —"

There was a muffled roar of rage from the house. They spun around just in time to see the back door burst open and crash against the wall. Someone hurtled out and began pounding across the grass towards them. Lief cried out in astonishment as he saw who it was.

It was the Ralad man!

"He is not drowned!" shouted Jasmine. "They saved him after all!" The relief in her voice made it clear that, however uncaring she had seemed, she had in fact cared, very much, about the little prisoner's fate. Already she was drawing her dagger and rushing to help him.

For now he needed help more than ever. Jin and Jod were after him, bursting through the door, screaming with rage. Jin had caught up an axe, and Jod was holding the long pole out in front of him, savagely swinging it from side to side as he ran. With every swing, the hook at the end, still dripping with slime from its dunking in the quicksand, missed the fleeing Ralad man by a hair. Any moment it might reach its mark.

Lief drew his sword and ran forward, leaving Barda standing, swaying, by the rock. He did not spare a thought for his own danger. The Ralad man's danger was too clear and urgent for that.

Jasmine's darting attacks were not slowing Jin and Jod down at all. The point of her dagger seemed to bounce off their leathery skin, and they were barely glancing at her. They were spitting with fury, and plainly far more interested in killing the Ralad man than in fighting anyone else.

It was as if the very sight of him filled them with rage. As if they knew him.

The little man was closer now. Panting in terror, he was desperately waving Lief back, pointing towards the leaves on the quicksand by the big rock and then to his own legs.

Lief realized that they had been wrong in thinking that he had fallen into the quicksand. Mud and slime coated his legs to the knees, but above that he was perfectly dry and clean. Somehow he had crossed the moat — perhaps at this exact spot.

He knows this place, Lief thought. He has been here before.

Two clear pictures flew into his mind. The cruel collar around the Ralad man's neck. The bed of moldy straw and the frayed rope in the monsters' kitchen.

And suddenly he was sure that the Ralad man had once slept on that straw, and that the collar he wore was once attached to that rope. Not long ago, he had been a prisoner of Jin and Jod. He was too small to be worth eating, so they had made him their slave. But at last he had escaped, only to be caught by the Grey Guards.

Lief, Jasmine, and Barda had left him asleep among the sweetplum bushes. He must have awoken, found himself alone, and guessed what had happened. Or perhaps he had even been roused by the shouting, and watched their capture from the bushes.

He rang the bell and threw a heavy rock into the quicksand, to lure Jin and Jod away from the house. Then he ran around to the other side of the house and crossed the moat. He returned to this terrible place, when he could have run away to safety. Why?

There could be no reason except to try to save the friends who had saved him.

Lief was only a few steps away from the running figures now. He sprang to one side, signalling to Jasmine to do the same. His mind was racing. His plan was to wait his chance, then leap between the monsters and their victim. He doubted that he and Jasmine could do more than wound them — but that, at least, would give the little man a chance to escape.

For that was the most important thing now. Not just for the Ralad man, but for them all. The small, running man with the muddy feet was the only one who could save them. Only he could tell them the way across the quicksand. Only he could tell them which of the floating leaves were safe to tread upon, and which were not.

Lief thought of the leaves as he had seen them, their strange red markings showing clearly against the shining, pale green background. Then, suddenly, he gasped.

"But he has already told us!" he exclaimed aloud.

Startled, the Ralad man glanced in his direction and stumbled. The great curved hook caught him around the waist, stopping him short and driving all the breath from his body. Jod screamed in triumph and began to pull him in.

But at the same moment Lief's sword came crashing down on the pole, cutting it through. Off balance and taken by surprise, Jod fell backwards, crashing into Jin. They went down in a tangle of lumpy, heaving flesh.

Jasmine sprang for them, her dagger raised.

"No, Jasmine!" shouted Lief, snatching the Ralad man from the ground and heaving him over his shoulder. "Leave them!"

He knew that now that he had discovered the secret of the stepping stones, speed would be far more likely to save them than fighting would.

Jin and Jod were clumsy, but very strong. If either Lief or Jasmine were wounded, it would be disastrous. The Ralad man was helpless, and Barda nearly so. They would both need help if they were to survive.

He began running back towards the rock, where Barda was anxiously waiting. After a moment's hesitation, Jasmine followed, shouting after him. He ignored her until they had reached Barda's side. Then he turned to her, panting.

"You are mad, Lief!" she cried angrily. "Now we are trapped with our backs to the quicksand! It is the worst possible place to stand and fight!"

"We are not going to stand and fight," gasped Lief, pulling the Ralad man more firmly onto his shoulder. "We are going to cross to the other side."

"But which leaves are we to trust?" Barda demanded. "Which mark the path?"

"None of them," panted Lief. "The spaces between them are the path."

He peered over Jasmine's head and his heart thumped as he saw that Jin and Jod were already scrambling to their feet. "Jasmine, you go first!" he urged. "Then you can help Barda. I will follow with the Ralad man. Make haste! They will be upon us at any moment!"

But Barda and Jasmine just gaped at him.

"The spaces between the leaves are quicksand!" Jasmine shrilled. "You can see it. If we leap upon it we will sink and die!"

"You will not die!" Lief panted desperately. "You will die if you leap anywhere else! Do as I say! Trust me!"

"But how do you know it is safe?" mumbled Barda, rubbing his hand over his brow as he tried to clear his head.

"The Ralad man told me."

"He has not said a word!" Jasmine protested.

"He pointed to this spot and then to his legs," shouted Lief. "His legs are muddy to the knees. But the leaves have not been trodden down into the mud in the last hour. They are quite clean and dry."

Still Barda and Jasmine hesitated.

Jin and Jod were coming. Jin's green-white, bristled face was so swollen with rage that her tiny eyes had almost disappeared. Yellow tusks jutted from her open, shrieking mouth. She was rushing towards them, the axe raised high, ready to strike.

Lief knew there was only one thing he could do. He took a breath and, holding the Ralad man tightly, jumped straight for the first gap between the leaves.

He plunged straight through the green slime. With a stab of panic he wondered if he had been wrong. He heard Jasmine and Barda crying out in horror. But then, at last, his feet touched flat rock. He had sunk only to his ankles.

With an effort he wrenched his right foot free and stepped to the next gap. Again he sank to his ankles. But again he touched firm ground.

"Come on!" he shouted over his shoulder, and with relief heard Barda and Jasmine leaping after him.

Jin and Jod squealed in fury. Lief did not turn to look. The muscles of his legs strained as he wrenched each foot free of the sucking quicksand to move on. Another step. Another . . .

And finally there was only the opposite bank ahead of him. Grass. Trees towering above. With a final, huge effort, he jumped. His feet hit solid earth and, sobbing with relief, he fell forward, feeling the weight of the Ralad man rolling from his shoulder.

He crawled to his hands and knees and turned to

look. Barda was close behind him. He was about to make the jump for the shore.

But Jasmine had stopped just behind him. She was crouching, slashing at something with her dagger. Had her foot become caught in a plant root? What was she doing?

The monster had not yet reached the edge of the moat, but Jin had raised the axe over her head. In terror, Lief realized that she was going to throw it.

"Jasmine!" he screamed.

Jasmine looked around and saw her danger. Like lightning, she stood, twisted, and jumped for the next stepping stone. The axe hurtled, spinning, towards her. It caught her on the shoulder just as she landed. With a cry she fell to her knees, slipping off the stone hidden under the green slime, toppling into the quicksand beyond. Greedily, it began to suck her down.

10 ~ Quick Thinking

Barda turned, swaying. He bent and caught Jasmine's arm, trying to haul her up beside him. But he was too weak to do more than stop her sinking further.

Howling in triumph, Jin and Jod lumbered forward. Any moment they would reach the big rock. And then . . .

"Leave me!" Lief heard Jasmine scream to Barda. "Take Filli — and leave me."

But Barda shook his head, and Filli clung grimly to her shoulder, refusing to move.

Desperately, Lief looked around for something he could hold out to them, to pull them in.

A tree branch, a vine . . . but there were no vines, and the branches of the trees here were thick and grew high off the ground. Never could he cut one in time. If only they had not lost their rope in the Forests of Silence! They had lost everything there. All they had were the clothes they wore . . .

Their clothes!

With a gasp of anger at his own slow wits, Lief tore off his cloak. He ran to the edge of the quicksand, twisting and knotting the soft fabric so that it made a thick cord.

"Barda!" he shouted.

Barda turned a white, strained face to look at him. Holding tightly to one end of the twisted cloak, Lief threw the other. Barda caught it.

"Give it to Jasmine!" shouted Lief. "I will pull her in!"

Even as he spoke, he knew the task was almost hopeless. Jin and Jod had reached the big rock. They were jeering, gathering themselves to spring. In moments they would be on the stepping stones, reaching for Jasmine, pulling her back towards them, tearing the cloak from Lief's hands. He would not be able to resist them.

Then, suddenly, like a miracle, a shrieking black shape plunged from the sky, straight for the monsters' heads.

Kree!

Jin and Jod shouted in shock as the black bird attacked them, its sharp beak snapping viciously. It wheeled away from their flailing arms and dived again.

Lief heaved on the cloak with all his might. He felt Jasmine's body move slowly towards him through the quicksand. Too slowly. Kree's attack was continuing, but Jod was hitting at him with the broken pole now. Surely the bird could not survive for long.

Desperately, Lief pulled again, and then felt two hands close over his own. Barda had reached the bank and was adding his strength to the task. Together they heaved on the cloak, digging their heels into the soft ground. And as they heaved, Jasmine's body moved, coming closer and closer to the bank.

She was beyond the last of the pale leaves and almost within reach of the bank when Kree shrieked. The lashing pole had caught him on the wing. He was fluttering crazily in the air, losing height.

Howling like beasts, free from the bird's attacks at last, Jin and Jod leaped together onto the first stepping stone. Lief caught a glimpse of Jod's metal teeth, gnashing in furious triumph.

Soon they will have Jasmine, he thought in despair. They will have her, and they will have us, too. They know we could not leave her. They know we will come after her, if they drag her away . . .

But Jasmine had twisted her head to look over her shoulder. It seemed she was thinking only of Kree. "Kree!" she called. "Get to the other side! Make haste!"

The bird was dazed and in pain, but he obeyed

the call. He fluttered across the moat, one wing barely moving, his feet almost touching the green slime. He reached the bank and fell to the ground.

Lief and Barda hauled on the cloak, their arms straining. One more pull and Jasmine would be near enough for them to reach her. One more pull . . .

But Jin and Jod were charging across the moat towards them. The bright patches of green slime between the pale leaves marked their path clearly. They did not hesitate. Already they were almost in the center.

As Lief watched in horror they lunged forward once more, roaring savagely, their clawed hands reaching for their prey.

And then their faces changed, and they shrieked. Their feet had plunged through the green slime — but found no safe ground beneath. Bellowing in shock and terror, they sank like stones, their arms thrashing frantically as their great weight drove them down.

And in seconds it was all over. The horrible screams were smothered. They were gone.

Dazed and trembling, Lief reached out and grasped Jasmine's wrist. Barda took the other, and together they dragged her up onto the bank. Her injured shoulder must have given her great pain, for she was white to the lips, but she did not murmur.

"What happened?" Barda gasped. "How did they sink? There were stepping stones there — we trod on them ourselves! How could they vanish?"

Jasmine managed a grim smile. "The stepping stones did not vanish," she muttered. "They are under the leaves I cut and moved. The monsters trod in the wrong places — the places where the leaves were floating before. I knew they would be too stupid, and too angry, to notice that the pattern had changed. They just went from one bright green patch to the next, as they always had."

Lief stared at the moat. He had not noticed the change to the leaf pattern, either. Even now he could not quite remember exactly how it had been.

Wincing with pain, Jasmine pulled out the tiny jar that she wore attached to a chain around her neck. Lief knew what the jar held: a little of the Nectar of Life that had cured Barda when he was injured in the Forests of Silence.

He thought that Jasmine was going to use it on her gashed shoulder, but instead she crawled to where Kree lay. The black bird struggled feebly on a patch of bare, sandy earth, his beak gaping and his eyes closed. One wing was spread out uselessly.

"You did not go home, wicked Kree," Jasmine crooned. "You followed me. Did I not tell you there would be danger? Now your poor wing is hurt. But do not fear. Soon you will be well."

She unscrewed the lid of the jar and shook one drop of the golden liquid onto the broken wing.

Kree made a harsh, croaking sound and blinked his eyes. He moved a little. Then, all at once, he stood up on his feet, fluffed his feathers, and spread both wings wide, flapping them vigorously and squawking loudly.

Lief and Barda laughed with pleasure at the sight. It was so good to see Kree well and strong again — and just as good to see Jasmine's radiant face.

There was a muffled sound behind them and they turned to see the Ralad man sitting up, blinking in confusion. His patch of red hair stood up like a crest. His eyes stared wildly around him.

"Do not fear, my friend!" cried Barda. "They are gone. Gone forever!"

Lief left them and went to Jasmine. She was sitting on the grass beside the sandy patch of earth, with Filli chattering in her ear. They were both watching Kree soaring and diving above them, testing his wings.

"Let me use the nectar on your shoulder, Jasmine," Lief said, sitting down beside her.

The girl shook her head. "We must save the nectar for important things," she said briefly. She dug in her pocket and brought out the jar of cream with which she had treated the Ralad man's wrists and ankles. "This will do for me," she said. "The wound is not serious."

Lief wanted to argue with her, but decided he would not. He was beginning to learn that it was best to allow Jasmine to do things her own way.

The shoulder was badly bruised. Now it was

swollen and angry red. Soon it would be deep purple. The wound in the center of the bruise was small, but deep. The corner of the axe blade must have struck there.

As gently as he could, Lief smeared the wound with the strong-smelling green cream. Jasmine sat very still and did not utter a sound, though the pain must have been great.

Barda came up to them with the Ralad man, who nodded and smiled at them, then put the palms of his hands together and bowed.

"His name is Manus. He wishes to thank you for saving him from the Guards, and from Jin and Jod," Barda said. "He says he owes us a great debt."

"You owe us nothing, Manus," said Lief, smiling back at the little man. "You risked your life for us, too."

Manus bent and, with his long, thin finger, rapidly made a row of marks in the sand beside him.

" 'You saved me twice from death,' " Barda translated slowly. " 'My life is yours.' "

Manus nodded vigorously, and it was only then that Lief realized that he was unable to speak.

Barda saw his surprise. "None of the Ralads

have voices, Lief," he said gruffly. "Thaegan saw to that, long ago. It was when, out of spite and jealousy, she created the Lake of Tears from the beauty of D'Or. The Ralads of that time raised their voices against her. She — put a stop to it. Not just for them, but for all who came after them. There have been no words spoken in Raladin for a hundred years."

Lief felt a chill. What sort of mad, evil being was this sorceress? Then he thought of something else, and glanced at the silent quicksand. Somewhere in those depths lay Jin and Jod, their wickedness stifled forever.

How long would it be before Thaegan found out? A month? A week? A day? An hour? Or was she flying towards them, filled with rage, at this very moment?

Thaegan had stolen the voices of a whole people because they had dared to speak against her. What sort of horrible revenge would she take on Barda, Jasmine, and Lief, who had caused the deaths of two of her children?

Run! whispered a small, shuddering voice in his head. *Run home, crawl into your bed and pull the covers over your head. Hide. Be safe.*

He felt a hand touch his arm, and looked up to see Manus beckoning to him urgently.

"Manus is anxious to be well away from here before the sun goes down," Barda said. "He fears that Thaegan may come. We all need rest, but I have agreed that we will walk as far as we can before making camp. Are you ready?"

Lief took a deep breath, banished the whispering voice from his mind, and nodded. "Yes," he said. "I am ready."

11 – To Raladin

That night they slept under a cluster of sweet-plum bushes far away from any stream or path. None of them wanted to be seen by anyone who might tell Thaegan where they were.

They were cold and uncomfortable, for their clothes were still damp and stiff with mud and they could not risk lighting a fire. But still they fell asleep at once, exhausted by all that had befallen them.

Sometime after midnight, Lief stirred. Moonlight shone palely through the leaves of the bushes, making shadows and patches of light on the ground. Everything was very silent. He turned over and tried to settle to rest once more. But, though his body still ached with weariness, thoughts had begun chasing one another through his mind, and sleep would not come.

Beside him, Manus was sighing and twitching — tormented, no doubt, by dreams.

It was not surprising that it should be so. Using signs and the strange picture-writing of his people, Manus had told them that he had been a prisoner of Jin and Jod for five long years. He had been making his way from Raladin to Del when, lured from the path by the tempting scent of the sweetplum bushes, he had fallen into the quicksand and been captured.

Lief could not bear to think of the long misery that the little man had suffered since then. Barda's understanding of Ralad's writing was not complete — but still he could translate enough to tell the terrible story.

Manus had been forced to work like a slave, beaten, starved, and treated with terrible cruelty. Tied to the wall of the kitchen, he had been forced to watch helplessly as Jin and Jod trapped, killed, and ate victim after helpless victim. Finally he had escaped — only to be seized by the troop of Grey Guards when he was almost home, and forced to march back the way he had come.

For five years he had lived with fear and loathing in the company of wickedness.

No wonder his sleep was haunted by nightmares.

When Lief asked him how long the journey to Raladin would take, he had answered quickly, scribbling on the earth with his finger.

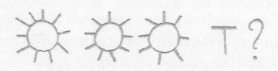

"Three days," Barda said heavily, looking at the marks. "If Thaegan does not catch us first."

If Thaegan does not catch us first . . .

Lief lay hunched on the ground and shivered as he thought of the letter "T" and the question mark. Where was Thaegan now? What was she doing? What orders was she giving?

The darkness of the night seemed to press in on him. The silence was heavy and menacing. Perhaps, even now, Thaegan's demons were stealing towards him like flickering shadows. Perhaps they were stretching out long, thin hands to clutch feet and ankles and drag him, screaming, away . . .

Sweat broke out on his forehead. A gasp of terror caught in his throat. He fought to stay still, not to wake the others. But the fear grew in him until he felt as though he must scream aloud.

The topaz protects its wearer from the terrors of the night . . .

He scrabbled under his shirt and pressed his shaking fingers against the golden gem. Almost at once the shadows seemed to shrink, and the terrible beating of his heart slowed.

Panting, he rolled onto his back and stared up through the leaves of the sweetplum bush. The moon was three-quarters of the way to full. Black against the starry sky was the proud shape of Kree, perched on the branch of a dead tree above them. The bird's head was up, and his yellow eyes shone in the moonlight.

He was not sleeping. He was alert. He was on guard.

Strangely comforted, Lief turned onto his side again. Only three days, he thought. Only three days to Raladin. And Thaegan will not catch us. She will not.

He closed his eyes and, still clutching the topaz, let his mind slowly relax into sleep.

✳

In the morning they set off again. At first they kept to small, well-hidden paths, but little by little they were forced into the open as the trees and bushes became less and the ground grew more parched.

They met no one. Now and again they passed houses and larger buildings where once grain had been stored or animals tended. All were deserted and falling into ruins. Some were marked with the Shadow Lord's brand.

At evening, as the light began to fail, they chose an empty house and set up camp there for the night. They filled their waterbags at the well and helped themselves to any food they found that was not spoiled.

They took other supplies, too, collecting rope, blankets, clothes, a small digging tool, a pot to boil water, candles, and a lantern.

Lief felt uneasy about taking things that belonged to others. But Manus, grieving at every sign of fear, destruction, and despair in the house, shook his head and pointed to a small mark scratched on the wall beside the window. It was the same mark he had made in the dust when he first saw them in the clearing.

He trusted them enough, now, to tell them what the mark meant. It was the Ralad sign both for a bird and for freedom. But it had spread far beyond Raladin, and had taken on a special meaning throughout Deltora. Carefully, Manus explained what the meaning was:

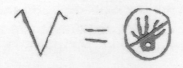

The freedom mark had become a secret signal used between those who had sworn to resist the tyranny of the Shadow Lord. By it they recognized one another — and told enemies from friends.

Before the owners of this deserted house had died or fled, they had left the mark for any future traveler of their kind to find. It was the only way they had of showing their defiance in defeat, and their hope for the future. It made Lief understand that they would have been glad to give anything they had to help the cause.

It was indeed fortunate that we found Manus, he thought. It is almost as if fate has brought us together for a purpose. As if our steps are being guided by an unseen hand.

He was half ashamed of the thought. Like his friends in Del, he had always jeered at such talk. But his journey had taught him that there were many things of which his friends in Del knew nothing, and many mysteries he was still to understand.

※

They moved on the next morning, and now that they knew what to look for they saw the freedom mark everywhere. It was chalked on crumbling walls and fences, marked out with pebbles on the ground, scratched into the trunks of trees.

Every time he saw it, hope rose in Lief. The sign was evidence that, however things were in the city of Del, in the countryside there were still people who were as willing as he was to defy the Shadow Lord.

Manus himself, however, was growing more and more serious and worried. The sight of the deserted countryside, the ruined houses, made his fears for his own village grow stronger with every step he took.

He had first left home, it seemed, when his people heard that the Shadow Lord wanted more slaves, and that his eyes were fixed on Raladin. The Shadow Lord had heard that the Ralads were hard workers of great strength and builders beyond compare.

Manus was to seek help from the resistance groups that the Ralads thought must exist in Del. They did not know that resistance in the city had been crushed long ago, and that their hopes of help were in vain.

Manus had been away over five years — years in which Thaegan had laid the land further to waste. He had no idea what he might find in Raladin.

But doggedly he moved on, hurrying despite his exhaustion. By the end of the third day it was all they could do to persuade him to rest for the night.

✳

Lief would long remember what happened the next morning.

They rose as dawn broke and left the cottage where they had taken shelter. Almost running, Manus led them across an open field and plunged into a patch of scrubby bushes beyond.

There was a small, deep pool there, fed by a little

stream that bubbled down from some gentle hills. Manus moved up the stream, sometimes splashing through the water, sometimes trotting along the bank. They followed, keeping up with difficulty, trying to keep his bobbing red top-knot in sight when he drew ahead.

He did not speak a word. All of them could feel his tension as he neared the place he had missed for so long. But when at last they reached a waterfall that cascaded in a fine veil from a sheet of rock, he stopped.

He turned and waited for them, his small face completely without expression. But even when they reached him, he did not move.

We have arrived, thought Lief. But Manus is afraid to go the last step. He is afraid of what he will find.

The silence grew long. Finally, Jasmine spoke.

"It is best to know," she said quietly.

Manus stared at her for a moment. Then abruptly he turned and plunged through the water-fall.

One by one the three companions went after him, shivering as icy water drenched them. There was darkness beyond — first the darkness of a cave, and then the greater darkness of a tunnel. And finally there was a soft glow in the distance that grew brighter and brighter as they moved towards it.

Then they were climbing through an opening on

the other side of the hill, blinking in the sunlight. A pebbled path ran down from the opening to a beautiful village of small, round houses, workshops, and halls, all simply but craftily made of curved, baked earth bricks. The buildings surrounded a square paved with large, flat stones. In the center of the square a fountain splashed, its clear, running water sparkling in the sunlight.

But there were no lights in the houses. Spiders had spun thick webs over the windows. The doors hung open, creaking as they swung to and fro in the gentle breeze.

And there was no other movement. None at all.

12 ~ Music

They trudged down the pebbled path to the village and began searching for signs of life. Lief and Jasmine looked carefully and slowly, their hearts growing heavier by the moment. Manus ran desperately into one house after another, with Barda pacing grimly behind him.

Every house was deserted. What had not been taken from inside had been destroyed.

When finally they met by the fountain in the square, the Ralad man's face was lined with grief.

"Manus thinks that his people have been taken to the Shadowlands, or are dead," Barda murmured.

"They may simply have moved away from here, Manus," said Lief. "They may have escaped."

The Ralad man shook his head vigorously.

"They would never have left Raladin willingly," said Barda. "It has always been their place."

He pointed at the piles of rubbish and the ashes of fires that dotted the streets and the square. "Grey Guards' leavings," he said, curling his lip in disgust. "They must have been using the village as a resting place for some time. And see how thickly the spider-web coats the windows. I would say that Raladin has been empty for a year or more."

Manus slumped onto the edge of the fountain. His feet kicked against something caught between a paving stone and the fountain edge. He bent and picked it up. It was a long flute, carved from wood. He cradled it in his arms and bowed his head.

"What are we to do?" whispered Lief, watching him.

Jasmine shrugged. "Rest for a day, then move on," she said. "We are not far now from the Lake of Tears. Manus will guide us the rest of the way, I am sure. There is nothing to keep him here."

Her voice was flat and cold, but this time Lief was not deceived into thinking that she cared nothing for the Ralad man. He knew now how well she cloaked her feelings.

Suddenly, a beautiful, clear sound filled the air. Startled, Lief looked up.

Manus had put the flute to his lips and was playing. His eyes were closed, and he was swaying from side to side.

Lief stood, spellbound, as the pure, running notes filled his ears and his mind. It was the most exquisite music he had ever heard, and the most heart-breaking. It was as though all the feelings of grief and loss that Manus could not speak aloud were pouring through the flute, straight from his heart.

Lief's eyes stung with tears. In Del he had never cried, fearing to be thought unmanly. But here and now, he felt no shame.

He could feel Barda, motionless beside him. He could see Jasmine nearby, her green eyes dark with pity. Filli was sitting bolt upright in Jasmine's arms, staring at Manus in wonder, and Kree was perched on her shoulder, still as a statue. All of them were caught and held, as he was, by the sound of Manus mourning his lost people.

Just then, behind Jasmine, in the corner of the square, Lief saw something move. He blinked furiously, thinking at first that his wet eyes were playing tricks. But there was no mistake. One of the huge paving stones was tilting!

He made a choking sound as a cry of alarm stuck in his throat. He saw Jasmine glance at him, startled, and turn to look behind her.

The stone was moving noiselessly from its place. Beneath it was a deep space glowing with warm light. Something was moving there!

Lief caught a single glimpse of a red-tufted head, and peering black button eyes. And then, with one, quick movement of a long-fingered, blue-grey hand, the stone was thrust completely aside. In moments, dozens of Ralads were clambering out into the open and rushing towards Manus.

Gaping in amazement, Lief turned and saw that exactly the same thing was happening at the other three corners of the square. Stones were sliding open and Ralad people were popping out of the holes beneath like corn from a hot pan.

There were dozens of them . . . hundreds! Adults and children of all ages. All of them were clapping, laughing, rushing to greet Manus, who had sprung up, dropping the flute, his face alight with joy.

✳

Hours later, bathed, filled with good food, and resting on soft couches of bracken fern and blankets, Lief, Barda, and Jasmine looked with wonder at what the Ralads had made in a few short years.

The cavern was huge. Lanterns filled it with soft light. There was a stream of water at one side, running into a deep, clear pool. Fresh, sweet air blew softly through pipes that ran through the chimneys of the houses above and opened to the sky. On the ground were cottages, storehouses, and a meeting hall. There were even streets and a central square like the one above their heads.

"What labor it must have been, to hollow out this cavern and make a hidden village here," Lief murmured. "It is like the secret tunnel their ancestors dug under the palace in Del. But so much larger!"

Barda nodded sleepily. "I told you the Ralads

were tireless workers and clever builders," he said. "And I told you they would never abandon Raladin. But even I did not suspect this!"

"And, plainly, Thaegan and the Grey Guards do not suspect it either," yawned Jasmine, who was lying back with her eyes closed. "The Guards camp above this very spot, with no idea that the Ralads are below."

"*We* had no idea, until they showed themselves," said Lief. "And they only did that because they heard the sound of the flute."

Jasmine laughed. She looked more peaceful than Lief had ever seen her. "It is good. The Shadow Lord must be very angry because the Ralads have slipped through his fingers. The more time the Guards take searching for them, the less time they will have to trouble us."

Lief watched Manus, who, surrounded by his friends, was still describing his adventures and the dangers he had faced since last seeing them. He was scribbling on a wall of the cavern with some sort of chalk, rubbing marks out almost as soon as he had written them.

"Do you think Manus will still lead us to the Lake of Tears?" he asked.

"He will," Barda murmured. "But not for a few days, I suspect. And that is good. It will force us to rest, and it is rest that we need, more than anything." He stretched lazily. "I am going to sleep," he announced. "It is still day, but who can tell down here?"

Lief nodded, but Jasmine made no reply. She was already asleep.

Soon afterwards, Manus turned away from the wall and went with his friends to the square in the middle of the cavern. All the Ralads seemed to be going there. Lazily, Lief wondered what they were doing, but in moments he understood.

Soft music filled the air — the sound of hundreds of flutes singing together of thankfulness, happiness, friends, and peace. The Ralads were celebrating the return of one they thought was lost. And Manus was among them, pouring into his own flute his heart's joy.

Lief lay still and let the music wash over him in waves of sweetness. He felt his eyelids drooping and did not fight it. He knew that Barda was right. For the first time in days they could sleep peacefully, knowing they were safe from harm and surprise. They should take all the rest they could while they had the chance.

❋

They passed three more days in Raladin. In that time they learned much about the Ralads and their life.

They learned, for example, that the little people did not stay below ground all the time. When it was safe, they spent their days outside. They tended the food gardens hidden nearby. They checked and repaired the pipes that brought air to the cavern and the alarms that alerted them when people approached the village. They taught the children to build and mend, and simply enjoyed the sunlight.

One thing they never did in the open was to play their music. They could not risk being heard. They played only underground, stopping immediately if the alarms warned them of intruders. It was a miracle that Manus had found the flute by the fountain. It had been lost and forgotten years ago, while the Ralads were still digging their hiding place in secret. It had lain in its place ever since, as if waiting for him.

On their fourth morning, the companions knew that it was time to leave. They were much stronger, well fed and well rested. Jasmine's wound had almost healed. Their clothes were clean and dry, and the Ralads had given each of them a bag of supplies.

They climbed to the surface with heavy hearts. They had no further reason to stay, but none of them wanted to go. This time of safety and peace had made the task ahead of them seem even more grim and terrifying.

Now, at last, they told the Ralads where they planned to go. Manus had told them to keep this secret for as long as they could, and now they found out why.

The people were horrified. They clustered around the travelers, refusing to let them pass, clutching Manus with all their strength. Then they began scribbling on the ground so fast that even Barda could not understand what they had written.

"We know the Lake of Tears is bewitched and forbidden," Lief told them. "We know we will face danger there. But we have faced danger before."

The people shook their heads in despair at their foolishness. Again they began scribbling on the ground — many, many signs of wickedness and death, with one sign larger than any other and repeated many times.

"What does that mean? What is it they especially fear?" whispered Lief to Manus.

Manus grimaced and wrote a single, clear word in the dust.

SOLDEEN

13 - The Lake of Tears

Jasmine frowned. "What is Soldeen?" she asked. But Manus could not, or would not, explain.

"Whatever this Soldeen is, we must face it," growled Barda. "As we must face Thaegan, if she pursues us."

The Ralads drew together at the mention of Thaegan's name. Their faces were very grave. Plainly, they thought the travelers did not understand their peril, and that meant that Manus was doomed to die with them, for he was determined to be their guide.

"Do not fear," Lief said grimly. "We have weapons. If Thaegan tries her tricks on us, we will kill her!"

The people shook their heads and scribbled again. Barda bent, frowning over the lines.

"They say she cannot be killed," he said at last, reluctantly. "The only way to kill a witch is to draw blood. And Thaegan's whole body is armored by magic. Many have tried to pierce it. All have failed, and died."

Lief glanced at Jasmine. Her eyes were fixed on Kree, who was flying high above them, stretching his wings.

Lief bit his lip and looked back at the Ralads. "Then we will hide from her," he told them. "We will hide, we will creep, we will do everything we can to avoid her notice. But we must go to the Lake of Tears. We must."

The tallest of the Ralads, a woman called Simone, stepped forward and scrawled on the ground.

"We cannot tell you why," said Barda. "But please believe that we do not go into danger out of reckless foolishness. We are pledged to a quest that is for the good of Deltora and all its people."

Simone looked at him keenly, then slowly nodded. And after that the Ralads stood aside and let the travelers walk down the narrow path that wound away from the village.

Manus led the way, his head high. He did not look back, but Lief did.

The people were standing very still, crowded together, watching them. Their hands were pressed to their hearts. And they did not move until the travelers were out of sight.

✳

By mid-afternoon the way had grown rough and the hills more rugged. Dead trees held bleached, white branches up to the pale sky. The grass crackled under the travelers' feet, and the low-growing bushes were dusty and dry.

There were scuttlings in the bushes, and rustlings in dark holes beneath the tree roots, but they saw no living creature. The air was heavy and still, and it seemed hard to breathe. They stopped for food and water, but sat only for a short time before moving on. The scuttling sounds were not pleasant, and they had the feeling that they were being watched.

As the sun sank lower in the sky, Manus began to walk more and more slowly, his feet dragging as though he was forcing them to move. His companions trudged behind him in single file, watching the ground which had become treacherous, filled with cracks and holes and littered with stones. They all knew, without being told, that they were nearing the end of their journey.

Finally, they came upon a place where the bases

of two steep, rocky hills met, making a narrow "V" shape. Through the gap they could see the red-stained sky and the fiery ball of the setting sun, glowing like a danger sign.

The Ralad man stumbled to a stop and leaned against one of the rocks. His skin was as grey as dust, his small black eyes were blank with fear.

"Manus, is the Lake — " Lief had not spoken for so long that his voice sounded like a croak. He swallowed, and began again. "Is the Lake just beyond these rocks?"

Manus nodded.

"Then there is no need for you to come any farther," said Barda. "You have guided us here, and that is all we ask of you. Go home now to your friends. They will be waiting anxiously for your return."

But Manus firmed his lips and shook his head. He took a stone and wrote on the rock.

This time Lief did not have to wait for Barda to read what the Ralad man had written. He had seen this message before. "You saved me twice from death. My life is yours."

He, Jasmine, and Barda all began to speak at once, but nothing they could say would change

Manus's mind. In fact, their arguments seemed to strengthen him. His breathing slowed, his color returned, and his dull eyes began to shine with determination.

At last, he decided to take action. He turned abruptly and almost ran to the gap between the rocks. In moments he had disappeared from view. They had no choice but to run after him.

They stumbled through the narrow passage in single file, keeping as close to the Ralad man, and to one another, as they could. So intent were they on their task that they were not prepared for what they saw when finally they reached the end of the pass.

Not far below them was a murky lake ringed by banks of thick, grey mud riddled with what looked like worm holes. In its center a slimy rock oozed water which dripped ceaselessly into the pool, causing slow, oily ripples to creep across its surface.

Twisted, barren peaks of clay rose beyond the lake like haunted things. There was not one green, growing thing to be seen. There was no sound but the dripping of water and the faint, squelching movements of mud. There were no smells but damp and decay. It was a place of bitterness, ugliness, misery, and death.

Lief's stomach churned. The Lake of Tears was well named. This, then, was what the sorceress Thaegan had made of the town of D'Or — the town that Jasmine had said was "like a garden." He heard Barda cursing softly beside him, and Jasmine hissing to Filli and Kree.

Manus simply stared, shivering, at the horror he had heard of all his life, but never seen. The demonstration of Thaegan's jealousy and wickedness. The evil that had caused his people to speak out, and receive a terrible punishment.

"Is the Belt warm?" Barda murmured in Lief's ear. "Does it feel the presence of a gem?"

Lief shook his head. "We must go closer," he whispered back.

Manus glanced at him curiously. They had spoken in low voices, but he had heard what they had said.

He has come this far with us, Lief thought. We must tell him something of what we are trying to do, at least. He will certainly find out in the end, if we are successful.

"We are searching for a special stone that we believe is hidden here," he told the Ralad man carefully. "But the matter is a deadly secret. If we find what we seek, you must tell no one, whatever happens."

Manus nodded, his hand on his heart.

Slowly they scrambled down the last of the rocks until they reached the mud that circled the Lake.

"This mud may not be safe," murmured Jasmine, remembering the quicksand.

"There is only one way to find out," Barda said,

and stepped forward. He sank to his ankles in the fine, grey ooze, but that was all.

Cautiously, the others joined him. Dropping the bags from their backs, they walked together to the edge of the Lake, their feet leaving deep holes where they trod. Lief crouched and touched the water with the tips of his fingers.

Immediately, the Belt around his waist warmed. His heart gave a great thud.

"The gem is here," he said in a low voice. "It must be somewhere under the water."

His ankle itched and absent-mindedly he put down his hand to scratch it. His fingers touched something that felt like slimy jelly. He glanced down and cried out with disgusted horror. His ankle was covered with huge, pale worms. Already they were swelling and darkening as they sucked his blood. He leapt up and kicked wildly, trying to shake them off.

"Be still!" shouted Jasmine. She sprang forward and caught Lief's foot in her hand. Her mouth twisted with distaste, she began pulling the squirming things off one by one, flicking them aside.

The swollen bodies scattered onto the grey mud and into the water, and Lief's stomach heaved as other mouths, other crawling hungers of every shape and size, coiled out of the ooze to snatch them up as they fell.

Suddenly the mud was alive with slimy things

twisting, creeping, slithering out of hiding. They fought for the worms, tearing them to shreds, and in seconds were winding around the travelers' feet and legs, wriggling eagerly upwards to find warm, bare flesh on which to feast.

Jasmine could help Lief no longer. Now his ears were ringing with her panic-stricken cries, and Barda's, as well as his own. Manus could not cry out. He was staggering, nearly covered by coiling shapes — shapes with no eyes, shapes that made no sound.

There was no hope. Soon they would be overwhelmed — eaten alive . . .

Filli screamed piteously. Kree, attacking from the air, tore at the beasts on Jasmine's arms, fighting as they coiled around his feet and wings, pulling him down.

Then, abruptly, as though on some sort of signal, the creatures froze. In their hundreds they began dropping to the ground and burrowing beneath the surface of the mud. In moments, they had all disappeared.

An eerie silence fell.

Shuddering all over, Jasmine began brushing frantically at her legs, arms, and clothes as if she still felt slimy things crawling over her body.

But Lief stood, dazed. "What happened?" he asked huskily. "Why . . . ?"

"Perhaps they do not like how we taste," said Barda, with a shaky laugh. He turned to give his hand to Manus, who had fallen to his knees in the churned mud.

It was then that Lief saw a trail of bubbles moving from the center of the Lake towards them. Moving fast.

"Barda! Jasmine!" he shrieked. But the warnings had no sooner left his mouth than the oily water beside them heaved and a huge, hideous creature rose from the depths.

Slime dripped from its skin. Its gaping mouth, lined with needle-sharp teeth, swirled with water, worms, and mud. Wicked spines sprouted, gleaming, from its back and sides and sprang like narrow spears from the flesh under its eyes, which burned with ravenous, endless hunger.

It lunged for them, throwing its body onto the shore with a hissing roar that chilled Lief's blood.

He knew that this was Soldeen.

14 ~ Soldeen

Lief stumbled back, frantically drawing his sword. Then he saw that Barda and Manus were the monster's chosen victims. They had fallen, and were frantically scrabbling in the mud, trying to escape. But Soldeen was almost upon them, his terrible jaws snapping shut and opening wide in an instant, like a huge, cruel trap.

Barely knowing what he was doing, Lief darted forward, shouting at the creature, plunging his sword into the vast, spiny neck.

The sword was torn from his hand as Soldeen swung around, the weapon still hanging, quivering, from his slimy hide. The blade was like a thorn to him — no more than a stinging irritation — but he was not used to defiance. He was angry now, as well as hungry.

He lunged at Lief, mouth agape. Lief leapt away — and sprawled heavily over the bags still lying on the mud where they had been dropped only minutes before.

He lay flat on his back, stunned. He heard Barda and Jasmine shrieking to him in terror, screaming at him to get up, to run!

But it was too late to run. And he had no weapon. He had nothing to protect himself from those terrible jaws, those needle teeth. Except . . .

He twisted and seized two of the bags by their straps. With all his strength he swung and threw them, straight into that gaping mouth, right to the back of the throat.

Soldeen reared back, choking for breath, shaking his great head from side to side. His tail lashed, churning the water to muddy foam. The sword flew out of his neck, turned in the air, and speared into the mud by Lief's foot.

Lief grasped it, sprang to his feet, and ran, ran for his life, shrieking for his companions to follow. He knew they had only moments to escape. Soldeen would swallow the bags, or cough them up, in no time.

Only when he reached the rocks did he look back. Barda was clambering up beside him with Manus in his arms. Jasmine, Filli, and Kree were close behind.

And Soldeen was sliding back into the Lake of Tears. He was sliding back into the murky depths, and disappearing from sight.

✳

Darkness came. They stayed upon the rocks, unwilling to move away from the Lake, though fearing another attack from the dark water at any moment.

Jasmine's supplies were gone, and Barda's also, for by chance it was their packs that Lief had thrown at Soldeen. The four companions huddled miserably together, sharing the blankets that remained and a damp meal that tasted of mud and worms. Slitherings, squelchings, and the sound of dripping water from the weeping rock set their nerves on edge.

As the full moon rose, flooding the Lake with its ghostly light, they tried to talk, to plan, to decide what they should do. If a gem was somewhere in the mud beneath that murky water, how could it ever be found?

They could return to Raladin for the proper tools and try to drain the Lake. But the work would take months, and none of them really believed that they would survive to complete it. Soldeen, the creatures of the mud, and Thaegan herself would see to that.

Two of them could try to lure Soldeen to the water's edge at one side of the Lake, while the other two dived for the gem on the other side. But in their hearts they all knew that such a scheme was doomed to failure. Soldeen would feel the movement in his waters, turn, and attack.

Gradually, as the hours crept by, they fell silent. Their cause seemed hopeless. The heavy sadness of the place had seeped into their very souls.

Remembering that the topaz was at its strongest at full moon, Lief put his hand upon it. Hope swelled in him as his mind cleared. But no great idea or wonderful knowledge came into his mind — only one fixed thought. They must at all costs fight this sadness. They must fight the feeling that they could never win, or defeat was certain.

They needed something that would lift them from their despair. Something to give them hope.

He turned to the Ralad man, who was sitting with his head bowed, his hands clasped between his knees.

"Play your flute, Manus," he begged. "Make us think of times and places other than this."

Manus looked at him in surprise, then fumbled in his bag and brought out the wooden flute. He hesitated for a moment, then put it to his lips and began to play.

Music rose in lilting waves, filling the dead air with beauty. The flute spoke of crystal-clear water trickling in cool shade, of birds singing in leafy green, of children playing and friends laughing, of flowers lifting their faces to the sun.

Lief felt as if a deadening weight was falling from his shoulders. He saw in the faces of Barda and Jasmine, and even in Manus himself, a dawning hope. Now they remembered what they were fighting for.

He closed his eyes, the better to feel the music. So he did not see the trail of bubbles breaking sluggishly on the surface of the Lake as something surged silently towards the shore.

But then, suddenly, the music stopped. Lief opened his eyes and looked in surprise at Manus. The Ralad man was rigid, the flute still held to his lips. His eyes, wide and glazed with fear, were staring straight ahead. Slowly, Lief turned to see what he was looking at.

It was Soldeen.

Muddy water poured from his back and slime dripped from the holes and lumps in his mottled skin as he slid onto the shore, forcing a great trough in the ooze. He was huge — far larger than they had realized. If he lunged for them now, he could reach them. He could crush them all with one snap of his terrible jaws.

And yet he did not attack. He watched them, waiting.

"Back!" Barda muttered under his breath. "Back away. Slowly . . ."

"DO NOT MOVE!" the hollow, growling command lashed out at them, freezing them to the spot.

Shocked, terrified, and confused, they stared, unable to believe that it was the monster who had spoken. And yet already he was turning his burning eyes to the trembling Manus, and was speaking again.

"PLAY!" he ordered.

Manus forced his lips and fingers to move. At last, the music began again, hesitating and feeble at first, but gaining in strength.

Soldeen closed his eyes. He was utterly still, poised half in and half out of the water. Like a hideous statue he faced them, while mingled mud and slime slowly dried on his skin in lumpy streaks.

Lief felt a light touch on his leg. Manus was nudging him with his foot, making signals with his eyes. *This is your chance to escape*, Manus's eyes were saying. *Climb up the rocks, move back through the pass, while he is distracted.*

Lief hesitated. Jasmine jerked her head at him impatiently. *Go!* her frown told him. *You have the Belt. You, at least, must survive, or all is lost.*

But it was too late. Soldeen's eyes had opened once more, and this time they were fixed on Lief.

"Why have you come to this forbidden place?" he growled.

Lief wet his lips. What should he say?

"Do not try to lie," Soldeen warned. "For I will know if you do, and I will kill you."

The music of the flute fluttered and stopped as if Manus had suddenly lost his breath.

"PLAY!" roared Soldeen, without moving his

gaze from Lief. Tremblingly, the Ralad man obeyed.

Lief made his decision. He lifted his chin. "We have come to seek a certain stone, which has special meaning for us," he said clearly, over the soft, wavering sound of the flute. "It was dropped from the sky, into this Lake, over sixteen years ago."

"I know nothing of time," hissed the beast. "But . . . I know of the stone. I knew that one day someone would seek it."

Lief forced himself to continue, though his throat seemed choked. "Do you know where it is?" he asked.

"It is in my keeping," growled Soldeen. "It is my prize — the only thing in this bitter and lonely place that comforts me in my misery. Do you think that I would let you take it, with nothing in return?"

"Name your price!" called Barda. "If it is within our power, we will pay it. We will go from here and find whatever — "

Soldeen hissed, and seemed to smile. "There is no need for you to search for my price," he said softly. "I will give you the stone in return for — a companion." He turned his great head to look at Manus.

15 - The Sorceress

L ief felt a chill run through him. He swallowed.

"We cannot — " he began.

"Give the little man to me," hissed Soldeen. "I like his face, and the music he makes. He will come into the Lake with me and sit upon the weeping stone. He will play to me through the endless days, the lonely nights. He will ease my pain, for as long as he lives."

Lief heard Jasmine draw a sharp breath and looked around. Manus had risen, and was stepping forward.

"No, Manus!" cried Barda, catching his arm.

Manus was very pale, but his head was high. He strained against Barda's grip.

"He wishes to join me," hissed Soldeen. "Let him come."

"We will not!" shrieked Jasmine, catching Manus

by the other arm. "He would sacrifice himself for us, but we will not allow it!"

"Give him to me, or I will kill you," growled Soldeen, the spines rising on his back. "I will tear you apart, and your flesh will be devoured by the creatures of the mud until there is nothing left but bones."

A wave of anger rose in Lief, burning like fire. He jumped up and threw himself in front of Manus, protecting him from the front, as Barda and Jasmine were protecting him at the sides. "Then do it!" he shouted, drawing his sword. "But if you do you will kill your companion, too, for you are too large to take one of us without the others!"

"WE SHALL SEE!" roared Soldeen, lunging forward. Lief braced himself for the attack, but at the last moment the beast twisted like a serpent, and three of the swordlike spines beneath his eyes ran under Lief's arm, tearing his shirt to ribbons and running through the folds of his cloak.

One easy toss of Soldeen's head, and Lief was jerked away from Manus and swung off his feet. For two terrifying seconds he dangled in midair, fighting for breath as the strangling ties of the cloak bit into his throat.

There was a roaring in his ears and a red haze before his eyes. He knew that in moments he would be unconscious. The cloak was double-tied, and he could not unfasten it. There was only one thing he could do. With the last of his strength he twisted, swung himself up, and caught one of the spines in his hands.

Immediately, the choking band around his neck loosened. Panting, he pulled himself up until he was sitting on the spine. He edged along it until he was just under the beast's eye.

His shirt had been torn away, and he shuddered at the feel of Soldeen's slippery, ridged hide on his bare skin. But still he clung there, pressing himself close, his sword steady in his hand.

"Drag me down into the mud and slime and drown me, if you will, Soldeen," he muttered. "But while we are gone my friends will escape. And I will plunge my sword into your eye before I die, I promise you. Will you enjoy life half-blind in this dank place? Or does your sight mean nothing to you?"

The monster was very still.

"Let our friend go, Soldeen," Lief urged. "He has suffered long, and only now is free. He came here for our sake. Make up your mind that we will not give him up. You shall not have him, whatever the cost!"

"You . . . would die for him," the beast growled, finally. "He . . . would die for you. And all of you would give up — everything — for your cause. I remember — I seem to remember — a time when I, too . . . long ago. So long ago . . ."

His eyes had narrowed. He had begun to sway, groaning and shaking his head.

"Something — is — happening to me," he

moaned. "My mind is — burning . . . clearing. I see — pictures of another time, another place. What have you done to me? What sorcery — ?"

And only then did Lief realize that the Belt of Deltora, and the topaz that it held, were pressing against the creature's skin.

"It is no sorcery, but the truth you see," he whispered. "Whatever you see — is real."

Soldeen's eyes gleamed in the moonlight, no longer the eyes of a ravenous beast, but those of a creature filled with unbearable suffering. And suddenly Lief remembered the golden eyes of the guardian of the bridge, and understood.

"Help us, Soldeen," he whispered. "Let Manus go free, and give us the stone. For the sake of what you once were. For the sake of what you have lost."

The tortured eyes darkened, then seemed to flash.

Lief held his breath. Confused and afraid, Barda, Jasmine, and Manus pressed together on the rocks, not daring to move.

"I will," said Soldeen.

Lief felt the eyes of his friends upon him as Soldeen slid back into the Lake and moved away from the shore. He knew that his life hung by a thread. At any moment Soldeen might change his mind, grow impatient or angry, toss him into the oily water, tear at him in rage.

Then he felt something that made him forget fear

116

and doubt. The Belt of Deltora was warming on his skin. It sensed that another gem was near — very near.

Soldeen had almost reached the weeping rock. The water had worn deep cracks and holes in its smooth surface. Under the gentle light of the moon it looked like a woman with her head bent in sorrow, tears falling from between her hands. Lief's heart thudded as he saw, cupped in one of the hands, something that did not belong there.

It was a huge, dark pink gem. The dripping flow of water hid it completely from the shore. Even here, so close, it was very hard to see.

"Take it," hissed Soldeen.

Perhaps he was already regretting his promise, for he turned his head aside, as if he could not bear to watch, while Lief stretched out his hand and plucked the gem from its hiding place.

Lief drew his hand back from the rock, opened it, and stared at his prize. Then, slowly, his excitement changed to confusion. He had no doubt that this was one of the gems they had been seeking, for the Belt around his waist was so warm that his damp clothes were steaming.

But he could not remember that any of the gems in the Belt of Deltora were pink. Yet this stone was pink, indeed, and seemed to be growing paler in color as he looked at it.

Or was it just that the light had changed? A thin

cloud had covered the moon, so that it shone through a smoky veil. Even the stars had dimmed. Lief shivered.

"What is the matter?" growled Soldeen.

"Nothing!" Lief said hastily, closing his hand again. "I have the stone. We can go back."

He twisted and signaled to Barda, Jasmine, and Manus, clustered together on the rocks. He saw them raise their arms, and heard their shouts of triumph.

The emerald is green, thought Lief, as Soldeen turned to swim back to the shore. The amethyst is purple. The lapis lazuli is deep blue with silver dots like stars, the opal is all the colors of the rainbow, the diamond is clear as ice, the ruby is red . . .

The ruby . . .

Some words leapt into his mind. He could see them as clearly as if the page from *The Belt of Deltora* was open before him.

✝ **The great ruby, symbol of happiness, red as blood, grows pale in the presence of evil, or when misfortune threatens . . .**

The ruby is red, Lief thought. The ruby grows pale in the presence of evil. And when red pales, what is it but pink?

The gem in his hand was the ruby, its rich color drained away by the evil of the Lake. But surely it had faded even more in the last few moments. Now it was no darker than the palm of his hand.

A terrible fear seized him. "Soldeen!" he cried. "We must — "

But at that moment, the sky seemed to split open with a jagged streak of light. With a fearful, rushing sound, a cloud of foul-smelling, yellow smoke belched through the crack, churning the Lake to mud and filling the air above it with thick, choking fumes.

And in the midst of the smoke, hovering above the water, was a towering figure, shining green, with wild, silver hair that crackled and flew around her beautiful, sneering face as though it was itself alive.

"Thaegan!" It was as though the whole Lake moaned the name. As though every creature, and even the rocks themselves, shrank and trembled.

The sorceress jeered.

She pointed the little finger of her left hand at Soldeen, and a spear of yellow light flew at him, hitting him between the eyes.

The beast cried out, twisting and rolling in agony. Lief was pitched violently sideways, and the great ruby flew from his hand, high into the air. He shouted in horror, snatching at it vainly even as he plunged towards the churning water of the Lake.

The gem made a great half-circle and began to fall. Gasping, struggling in the muddy foam, Lief watched in horror as it dropped into a deep crack in the weeping rock and disappeared from sight.

"You shall never have it!" cried Thaegan, her voice cracking with fury. "You — who have dared to enter my lands! You who have freed one of my creatures and made another do your will! You who have killed two of my children and mocked my power! I have followed you. I have smelt you out. Now, you will see!"

Again she raised her hand, and Lief felt himself being swept towards the edge of the Lake. Foul-smelling water rushed into his eyes, nose, and mouth. Nameless things, fighting for life as he was, battered against his face and body and were crushed.

Half-drowned, he was cast up on the shore. He crawled, coughing and choking, through the oozing mud and foam, only half aware that Barda, Jasmine, and Manus were running towards him.

They hauled him to his feet and began dragging him to the rocks.

But Thaegan was already there, barring their way, her silver hair flying in the smoke, her body shining green. "You cannot escape me," she hissed. "You will never escape."

Barda flung himself at her, his sword pointed straight at her heart. "One drop of your blood, Thaegan!" he shouted. "One drop, and you are destroyed!" But the sorceress laughed shrilly as the blade swerved aside before it touched her and Barda was flung back, sprawling, into the mud. Kree screeched as Jasmine leapt forward to take the big man's place, only to be thrown back with even greater force, tumbling over Lief and Manus, taking them both down with her.

They wallowed helplessly in the ooze, struggling to rise.

Thaegan grinned, and Lief's stomach heaved as her beautiful face shifted like a mask and he glimpsed the evil horror beneath.

"Now you are where you belong!" she spat. "At my feet, crawling in the mud."

Kree screeched again and flew at her, trying to beat at her with his wings. She turned to him, as if noticing him for the first time, and her eyes lit with greed.

"Kree!" screamed Jasmine. "Get away from her!"

Thaegan laughed, and turned back to face them. "The black bird I will save for my own delight," she snarled. "But you — you will know nothing of his pain."

Baring her teeth, she raked her victims with eyes full of hate and triumph. "You are to become part of my creation. Soon you will forget everything you have ever held dear. Sick with loathing at your own ugliness, feeding on worms in the cold and the dark, you will creep in the ooze and slime with Soldeen, forever."

16 - Fight for Freedom

Thaegan raised her left hand high above her head, fist tightly clenched. It gleamed, green and hard as glass. The yellow smoke swirled as Kree dived wildly, uselessly, around her head. Lief, Barda, Jasmine, and Manus staggered together, trying to run. Laughing at their terror, she lifted the little finger, ready to strike. Its tip, white as bone, gleamed through the dimness.

Like a black arrow, Kree hurtled from the smoke. With a vicious snap his sharp beak stabbed and stabbed again at the death-pale fingertip.

The sorceress shrieked in rage, shock, and pain, shaking the bird off, hurling him aside. But red-black blood was already welling from the wound on her fingertip and slowly dripping to the ground.

Her eyes widened, unbelieving. Her body shuddered and writhed and turned as yellow as the smoke that still hung about her. Her face became a hideous blur, melting and re-forming before her victims' horrified eyes.

And then, with a high, whistling hiss, she began to shrivel, to crumple, to collapse in upon herself like a rotting fruit left in the sun.

Face down in the mud, Lief wrapped his arms around his head to hide the ghastly sight, smother the terrible sound. He heard Soldeen bellowing in the Lake behind him, crying out in triumph or terror. Then, with a low, terrifying rumble, the earth began to shudder and heave. Icy waves pounded on his back as the waters of the Lake swelled and crashed upon the shore.

Terrified at the thought of being sucked back into the deep, he threw himself forward, dragging himself blindly through the spray. Dimly he could hear Jasmine and Barda calling to each other, calling to Manus and to him. His fingertips touched rock, and with a last, desperate effort he heaved himself out of the swirling mud onto firm ground. He clung there, the breath sobbing in his aching throat.

Then, suddenly, everything stilled.

His skin prickling, Lief lifted his head. Barda and Manus were lying near him, pale but alive. Jasmine crouched a little further away, with Kree on her wrist and Filli, soaked and bedraggled, in her arms. Where Thaegan had stood there was nothing but a yellow stain on the rock.

The sorceress was dead. Trying only to stop her from casting her spell, Kree had wounded her in the one place on her body that was not armored — the fingertip she used to work her evil magic.

But it was not the end. Something was about to happen — Lief could feel it. The clouds had disappeared, and the full moon flooded the earth with radiant white light. The very air seemed to shimmer.

And the silence! It was as though the earth had caught its breath. Waiting . . .

Slowly, Lief turned to look behind him.

The tempest had almost emptied the Lake. Now it was just a broad sweep of shallow water gleaming in the moonlight. A multitude of slimy creatures lay stranded in heaps around its edges and on its flattened banks.

Soldeen was in the center, by the weeping rock. He was motionless, his head upraised. He was staring at the moon as though he had never seen it before. As Lief watched, there was a long, whispering sigh. Then Soldeen simply — vanished, and standing in his place was a tall, golden man with a mane of tawny hair.

The weeping rock quivered, and cracked from top to bottom. The two halves crumbled away in a cloud of fine, glittering dust. A woman stepped from the shining cloud. She was golden, like the man, but her hair was black as night. In her hand, held high, was a huge, red gem.

Lief staggered to his feet. He wanted to shout, to

exclaim, to cry out in shock, disbelief, and joy. But he could not make a sound. He could only stare as the man and woman joined hands and together began to walk towards him, across the water.

And as they walked, looking around them with the wondering eyes of those who still cannot believe their happiness, everything began to change.

The earth dried and bloomed with grass and flowers under their feet. Color and life spread from their footsteps, carpeting the dead earth as far as the eye could see. Twisted stumps and bare rocks became trees of every kind. Clay fell in sheets from the ragged peaks, revealing shining towers, beautiful houses, and spraying fountains. The pure, sweet sound of bells rang through the air.

All around the margins of the Lake, creatures were dissolving and re-forming. Golden people were rising from the ground, dazed from their long sleep, murmuring, weeping, laughing. Birds were fluffing their feathers and taking flight, singing their joy. Insects were chirruping. Furred animals were looking about them and hopping, bounding, or scurrying into the grass.

Lief felt Barda, Jasmine, and Manus move to stand behind him. The man who had been Soldeen, and the woman who had shared his long, long suffering, were not far from them now, but still Lief could hardly believe his own eyes.

"Can it be true?" he murmured.

"If it is not, we are all dreaming the same dream," said a chirpy voice he did not know. He swung around to see Manus, grinning at him.

"Manus — you can speak!" His own voice cracked and squeaked in his astonishment.

"Of course! With Thaegan's death, all her spells have been undone," said Manus cheerfully. "The people of Raladin and D'Or will not be the only ones in these parts with reason to be grateful to your gallant black bird, believe me."

Perched proudly on Jasmine's wrist, Kree squawked and puffed out his chest.

"And grateful to you." The deep, quiet voice was new to Lief, yet there was something familiar in it. He turned to meet the steady, deep grey eyes of the man who had been Soldeen.

"We have met before as enemies," the man said. "Now, at last, we meet as friends." His grey eyes warmed. "I am Nanion. This — is my lady, Ethena. We are the chiefs of D'Or, and we owe you our freedom."

The woman smiled, and her beauty was like the beauty of a radiant summer sky. Lief blinked, dazzled. Then he realized that she was holding out her hand to him. Balanced in the palm was the ruby — richly glowing, deepest red.

"You have need of this, I think," she said.

Lief nodded, swallowing, and took the gem from

her hand. It warmed his fingers, and the Belt around his waist grew hot. Quickly he moved to unfasten it, then hesitated, for Manus, Nanion, and Ethena were watching.

"Your secret, if it is a secret, will be safe with us," Manus chirped. He cleared his throat, as if still amazed and startled by the sound of his own voice.

"It will," said Ethena. "For a hundred years we have lived a half-life that was worse than death, our land laid waste and our souls imprisoned. Because of you, we are free. Our debt to you will never be repaid."

Barda smiled grimly. "Perhaps it will," he said. "For if our quest succeeds, we will have need of you."

He nodded to Lief, and Lief took off the Belt and put it on the ground in front of him.

Manus gasped, his button eyes wide. But it was Nanion who spoke.

"The Belt of Deltora!" he breathed. "But — how do you have it, so far from Del? And where are the seven gems? There is only one!"

"Two, now," said Lief. He fitted the ruby into the medallion beside the topaz. It glowed there, scarlet against the shining steel. The ruby, symbol of happiness. Greedily, he drank in the sight.

But Ethena and Nanion had drawn close together, and their tawny faces were pale under the moon. "It has happened, then," Ethena murmured.

"What we feared. What Thaegan promised, before she sent us into darkness. The Shadow Lord has come. Deltora is lost forever."

"No! Not forever!" cried Jasmine fiercely. "Any more than D'Or was lost forever. Or you!"

Nanion stared at her, startled by her anger. Then, slowly, he smiled. "You are right," he said softly. "No cause is lost while brave souls live and do not despair."

Lief lifted the Belt and put it on. It felt heavier than before. Only a little — but enough to make his heart swell with happiness.

A clamor of shouting and singing arose from the valley. The people had seen Nanion and Ethena from afar and were running towards them.

Ethena put a gentle hand on Lief's arm. "Stay with us a while," she urged. "Here you can rest, and feast, and be at peace. Here you can regain your strength for the journey ahead."

Lief glanced at Barda, Jasmine, and Manus and read in their faces what he knew he would. D'Or was beautiful, and the air was sweet. But —

"Thank you," he said. "But we are expected — in Raladin."

They said their farewells and left Ethena and Nanion turning to greet their people. The sound of bells ringing in their ears, they climbed up the rocks, pushed their way through the gap, and began to trudge back the way they had come.

Happiness was behind them, and happiness was before them. They could only guess at the Ralads' joy.

A few days' rest, thought Lief. A few days of storytelling, laughing, and music, with friends. And then — another journey, another adventure.

Two gems were found. The third awaited them.